Legends of Wrath

FURY FALLS INN • BOOK 5

BETTY BOLTÉ

www.MysticOwlPublishing.com

Copyright © 2022 by Betty Bolté
www.bettybolte.com
Digital ISBN: 978-1-7354669-8-9
Paperback ISBN: 978-1-7354669-9-6

About

Legends of Wrath

Fury Falls Inn in 1821 Alabama. A place for ghosts, witches, and magic. A place of secrets and hidden dangers. A place where Silas Fairhope must rewrite his vengeful family's history to preserve its chance at a future.

Answering his sister's frantic summons, journalist Silas discovers not only life-changing concealed powers but also a ruthless witch hunter out to kill her along with two witches, his aunts, who'll stop at nothing to possess her powers. Silas uncovers the truth lurking in his deceased grandfather's twisted plans of fame and power. The aunts—both powerful, vindictive witches—seek to fulfill those evil plans with his sister's reluctant help. Can Silas rewrite the shocking truth of the family's deadly past before it's too late for them to have any future??

*To Carla Swafford for her encouragement and
friendship*

Dear Reader,

This story continues the series of six supernatural historical fiction stories set in 1821 northern Alabama. With each of these, I fully expect I'll discover more about the history of this state I call home.

I'd like to thank my beta readers—Sue, Alicia, Danielle, Crystal, Mandy, and Chris—who read a prepublication version of *Legends of Wrath* and provided invaluable feedback. I appreciate your time, observations, and suggestions for improving the story!

I'd also like to thank readers like you who continue to inspire me to write stories with joy and passion. I always enjoy hearing from my readers, so please drop me a line at betty@bettybolte.com any time.

If you enjoy this book, please subscribe to my newsletter via www.bettybolte.com to be informed of other books I'll write in the future. You can also learn more about me, my other existing books, and read excerpts of each book at my website. You may also enjoy learning more about the behind the scenes research and recipes included in this story at www.bettybolte.net.

Again, thanks for reading! I hope you enjoy *Legends of Wrath*.

Betty

Chapter One

Northern Alabama, October 1821

The foothills stretched away from the wide, rutted dirt road along which Silas Fairhope trotted his bay-colored Morgan horse. He only had to ride a short while farther to finally see his beloved, estranged sister Cassandra. Keeping his eyes peeled for the turn up the lane leading to the Fury Falls Inn, he posted with the movement of his sturdy gelding. Everywhere he stopped at a tavern or inn, the people had known of the renowned inn. Many had seemed envious of his destination. What would he find there? He could sense his sister's eagerness, through a surprising new ability he'd discovered but couldn't explain, where they could connect silently with their minds. The link grew stronger as he neared the turn. Anticipation of reuniting with her filled him with joy.

Suddenly, a figure dressed in black burst into the road from the yard of a cottage off to one side. Silas pulled hard on the reins to avoid running over the fleeing man, his horse rearing and then dropping back to the ground. The man's sense of success and glee coupled with an underlying fear invaded Silas's chest. As the horse settled beneath him, Silas peered in the direction from which the man had come to try to determine the atmosphere of the quaint abode. The thatched roof, dark windows, and scraggly front yard seemed to hunch against the surrounding forest. His probing was met with silence and sadness.

He swiveled his head to stare at the empty road. What was the man running from?

Dare he investigate?

No. He shouldn't. He didn't know anyone in these parts. Nor did he desire to become involved in anything nefarious. He only wanted to see his sister and brothers for the first time in years. Someone else, like the local sheriff, would need to find out what had caused that man to run. Surely, it was none of his business as a complete stranger.

Relieved with his rationalization, he urged his horse into a trot again. After a few minutes he espied the lane he sought and urged his bay into a canter. His active imagination made him wonder about the mystery he left behind. He'd probably never discover the answers to the many questions in his head. Questions his writer's curiosity demanded answers to. However, his boss had not assigned him to investigate and report on what he found. No. Better to stick with his mission of answering his sister's summons, of journeying to the inn like his other three brothers before him. Besides, he simply couldn't wait to once more embrace his beloved sister.

Notes of a familiar song drifted through the open front doors to rest uneasily on her ear. Cassie Fairhope paused in arranging flowers in the vase in the entrance hall of the Fury Falls Inn, unease blending with a growing sense of danger. A fair fall day allowed for the windows and doors to stand open to the fragrant flow of air. Air which also carried the sounds of a busy place: horses clomping up the carriageway, men greeting each other with a shout and a laugh, cows mooing in their field by the stable, dogs barking at approaching carriages and coaches. Sifting through the other sounds, Cassie detected the strum of a guitar and sensed in her core her oldest brother probing her emotions, checking to assess her comfort or concern. With a final glance and tweak at the arrangement of red mums, cattails, and various fronds, she wiped her hands on her apron as she stepped onto the wide front porch.

Giles Fairhope, her brother and the family's Guardian, relaxed on a chair with his guitar in his lap. He picked out an opening set of notes, then settled into strumming the strings with strong and reverent hands. She soon found herself humming along with him. His version of her song, the one she'd written as a first attempt at crafting a calming spellsong. She liked the tune just fine, but the lyrics... they left a lot to be desired.

She'd struggled with the words because what she held in mind didn't flow to the page. She wanted something she could sing that wouldn't reveal her intent to calm another's agitation. More of a ballad she could infuse with her will. A gentle story to encourage the listener to relax and be open to suggestion. In other words, generic enough to entertain and yet allow her to work her magic.

The guitar fell silent, drawing her attention.

"Why'd you stop?" She crossed in front of him to slip around the small table and settle onto the matching chair.

"It sounds fine."

He shrugged and rested his large hand on the curved body of the instrument. "Do you mind that I chose to play your song?"

"Not at all. Maybe it will even help. I wrote it as a calming song, but I like what you did with the tempo so I may copy that idea." She leaned back in her seat but couldn't relax. Alert and tense, she scanned the area in front of the popular roadside inn. Beside her, Giles also tensed and set his guitar on the floor, leaning the gleaming wooden instrument against the table. She glanced at him, catching the look of concern in his expression. "You feel it, too?"

He nodded but kept his gaze moving. "I had hoped it was just me being too on edge, or rather that I was sensing you're on edge. But now that you're right here, it seems even more apparent."

Cassie closed her eyes to concentrate entirely on reaching out to sample the emotions of the other people close by. Relatively speaking, given she could now sense emotions from miles away. At first, she'd only sensed others' emotions standing nearby. But each time her brothers showed up, her powers increased. Most of the business and working men stomping in and out were intent on their own needs and desires. But among them, some number of others kept close watch on her activities. She reached out farther and a flare of joy filled her heart. Her final brother, Silas, neared and should arrive in a matter of minutes. Then all four of her brothers would have answered her plea to come to the inn, to come to her aid after the murder of their mother while their father was away on business. Little did she know when she wrote those letters months ago that she'd be faced with both a killer on the loose and two demanding aunts who insisted she unite with them. Something she would not and could not do.

Soon their father would also arrive, bringing the commissioned furniture. Then the family would finally be together again. Even their mother lingered as a ghost, waiting for something Cassie wasn't clear on. Yet this sense of urgency, a hint of danger growing, drifted on the autumn breeze. The sensation rattled around inside her like a neglected bean in a tin can.

Giles stood and paced to the edge of the porch, propping a hand on a support pole. "I can tell you're sensing the threat, because you're very uneasy."

"I feel like I'm being watched all the time. By more than one pair of eyes." She shivered as the sense of danger inched higher. She longed for her father to return because he was her only hope of putting an end to this threat. Her ghostly ma told her he would know what to do. Surely, a powerful warlock like him could quell the dangers swirling about the inn. Could stop the killer with his powers, and persuade her aunts to stop haranguing her. If he couldn't, then what?

"It's the witch hunter I bet. He's probably growing impatient and desperate to finish his apparent intent to annihilate witches around here." Giles spun around to stalk toward her, stopping when he stood a foot in front of her shoe tips. "He's employed others to do his dirty work. That's what you're sensing, the others who are waiting for their opportunity. Don't give it to them."

Having his large, muscular frame looming over her, casting her in his shadow, deepened her unease. She stood and met his intense gaze. Better to be on her feet, able to react more quickly. "What do you propose I do?"

She studied him, anticipating from recent experience what he'd ask. A guard or chaperone to be with her at all times. Poor Teddy had tried his best, but the young boy couldn't deter the attack she'd already fought off.

"I'm going to stay close to you as much as possible. If I can't be with you, then you stay inside and away from strangers. Can you do that?"

She blinked at him, counting to five as she struggled to not lash out at him. Not again. Her muscles ached from a bow-string tension. She forced herself to relax. "I refuse to be a prisoner in my own home, Giles. With all of my brothers here along with Flint, surely I'm safe on this property."

"I know your fiancé will try to protect you, Cassie, but he is limited to mortal means. Please, keep me or one of our other brothers with you at least. You shouldn't be alone. Ever. We can use our abilities to ward off anyone who might threaten you bodily."

What more might the mysterious attackers threaten her with? They'd tried to kill her twice now, both attempts thwarted. She'd grown stronger, more capable of defending herself. She needed space, air. She paced away from Giles, staring out at the people coming and going in the front yard of the inn.

Footfalls on the floorboards behind her had her spinning around, fear spiking. Her hand flew to her throat, sparking in preparation of throwing off an attacker. No need. She swallowed and drew in a deep breath. "You scared me."

"My apologies." Flint tucked a newspaper under one arm as his smile wilted into a worried frown. "What's the matter?"

"Nothing." If she told him, then he'd agree with Giles and demand she stay inside. She had no inclination toward hiding or walking around afraid every minute. "Giles was just...showing me a different way to play one of my songs."

"Cassie, tell him the truth." Giles took two steps toward them. "He must know."

"Know what?" Flint's eyes narrowed as he searched her expression. "Are you all right?"

"I'm fine, thank you. It's only a feeling I have." She glanced at her brother when he cleared his throat meaningfully. "A feeling *we* have. Satisfied?"

"Go on." Giles crossed his arms over his muscular chest. "You shouldn't keep secrets. You know how upset you were about all the ones Ma and Pa kept from us."

She rolled her eyes at him and then peered up at her fiancé's concerned expression. Giles was right. Flint deserved to know all of it despite her preferences. "We're sensing an increasing number of people who mean me harm. Giles wants to play guardian angel and be with me all the time, but I don't think it's actually necessary. Not in my own home."

Flint's expression turned stony. Then he pulled the paper free and unrolled it, only to roll it back into a tube. "The thing is, sweetheart, we have people, men, coming and going all day long. Most we know, but not all of them. Giles is right to worry." Flint tapped the paper on his palm with a nod of mutual understanding at Giles then slid his gaze back to Cassie. "I agree with him."

"I knew you would." She heaved a sigh and let it out. "I will try to comply."

"Promise me." Flint jabbed the paper under one arm then pulled her close, lightly kissing her lips. "Please."

When he put it that way, what else could she do? "I promise."

"Thank you." Flint kissed her again, and then tilted his head as he contemplated her. "Do you know when your other brother, Silas, will arrive?"

She smiled up at him as she reached out again, trying to measure distance in emotional strength. "He's very close."

"It will be good to see him." Giles dropped his arms to his sides and moved to pick up his guitar. "Want to help me remember the rest of that song, Cassie? I think I've got it muddled in my memory."

"Of course." Cassie took a step toward the table and then turned back to Flint. "Did you need me for anything?"

Flint shook his head and gestured toward the vacant seat. "Go ahead. I'll go inside to prepare for the afternoon rush. See you later." With that, he tipped two fingers to his brow toward Giles and then strode through the open doors.

Cassie resumed her seat, raising her inner barrier so she could concentrate on the calming songspell instead of the emotions swirling around her. Listening to Giles pick out the tune Greensleeves, she hummed along and then broke out into singing the words. When Giles stumbled, she continued the tune so he could pick up what he'd forgotten.

When life seems hard and oh so wrong
And nothing goes so easily
Don't fret and pine for days gone by
But hold to love and let it be.

Soft, soft be still and calm
Softly lay down your burdens.
Hush, hush now let things be

And trust in home and family.

Though storms may rage beyond these walls
And lightning flash across the sky
Within is calm and all is well
Our care and sweet love will brave the night.

Soft, soft be still and calm
Softly lay down your burdens.
Hush, hush now let things be
And trust in home and family.

When they'd finished the entire song, she smiled at him. "That's lovely. You should accompany me in the dining room. We could be famous."

He guffawed as he leaned on the guitar. "I don't know about that. Maybe infamous."

She chuckled but the idea took root. Her mother had once mentioned that if witches joined forces their magic became stronger. Would it work with her Guardian's strength and playing his guitar to strengthen her voice's effect on others? "I'm serious. I think the guests would enjoy having both of us play for them. You won't have to sing if you don't want to. Please?"

He stared at her for several moments and then slowly shook his head. "Are you sure?"

"Definitely. We'll be brilliant." And stronger together, with any luck.

Golden rays of sunshine alternated with long dark

streaks of shadows up the lane as Silas rode toward the Fury Falls Inn. Cassie anticipated his arrival. He sensed her eagerness as well as her anxiety. How he was able to sense what she felt, or anyone else for that matter, he didn't fathom. He'd awoken one morning several months previous and found he was aware of what others felt, whether he wanted to know or not. After some trial and error involving blanking his mind and pushing away all of his own feelings, he'd managed to control when he let others in. Thank goodness. Those first weeks had seemed like a lifetime in purgatory. How long the unwanted ability would plague him remained an open question.

The inn nestled at the edge of a forest blanketing the mountains beyond. He'd heard of the wilderness of these parts but he'd not had reason to venture out to experience the area for himself. Seeing the foothills bedecked in the colors of autumn gave them a warmth he didn't feel. He sensed an uneasy peace, as if it held its breath.

Men in work clothes and fine suits dismounted from their horses or emerged from fine horse-drawn vehicles to head inside the two-story stone and red-brick structure. Looked like a new wooden section had recently been added, the wood fresh and glowing in the late afternoon sunlight. He scanned the oak shake-shingled roof, noting several chimneys, and then noticed a strange shimmery blur at the right end of the roof. He rubbed his eyes and looked again. Gone. He must be more tired than he realized. He slowed his mount from a canter to an energetic walk, taking a moment to survey the property his sister called home.

He rode past a gazebo off to his right, draped in vines preparing to doze through the coming winter. Ahead, the inn comprised two buildings connected by a covered passage and wrapped with porches to create a welcoming edifice. He'd visited many fine establishments over the last several years, and this one could hold its own. Not a fancy place, but the atmosphere suited the kind of inn he imagined he'd find inside. Wide double doors on the left part with a table and two cushioned rocking chairs beside it seemed to be the public tavern as so many people came and went through the open doors on this fine fall afternoon. He suspected the quieter right side was the family residence. He halted at one of two hitching rails and swung out of the saddle, the leather creaking as he dropped with a thud to the crushed stone. He tied his horse to the rail and turned to mosey on inside, only to have a girl launch herself into his startled embrace.

"Silas!" Cassie hugged him hard for a moment and then composed herself, standing demurely smiling up at him. "Welcome to the inn."

"What a surprising and energetic welcome, too. You've certainly grown." He scanned her head to toe, seeing how much of a young woman she'd become. "I'm glad to see you again."

The curvy young woman smiling up at him looked little like the blond, blue-eyed girl she'd been as a child. Long curls bounced about her straight shoulders. Energy and sparkle emanated from within, lighting her eyes. A slightly twisted front tooth, the result of a childhood fall, endeared her pleasant countenance to him all the more. Making her appear human despite the ethereal quality surrounding her. Despite her being younger than him, Silas had looked up to her. Her thoughtfulness, caring, and teasing all blended into the upbeat person she'd become. How he'd missed being with his sister, seeing her grow and mature into such a fine lady.

He'd been separated from his family for years. Spent most of that time in the company of strangers, interviewing them and learning about the places they called home or their places of employment. He'd write up a pithy description, include a few quotes, and mail his article back to his boss in Boston. Weeks later, he'd receive a clip from the newspaper his work had appeared in, which he'd add to the slowly expanding packet in his saddlebags. His most prized possessions resided within the leather walls of battered bags. Always on the road, he didn't have anywhere else to keep them.

"I'm so glad you're finally here. I've missed you so much." Cassie hugged him again and then stepped back, brushing her long skirts with her hands.

"It's been a long time, but I'm here now." Silas blinked as her worry flashed through him, then it was gone. Had he imagined it? Or had she shielded herself from others detecting her feelings? Protecting himself proved a useful thing to know how to do. "Are you here alone? Where's Pa?"

She shook off his question with a half-smile. "Come in. We'll take care of your tired horse for you." She looked toward the stable and motioned toward a lanky boy emerging from the shadowy interior. "Liam, come see to this horse."

The youth trotted across the carriageway and led Silas' bay back from where he'd come. Silas detected fatigue in his faithful horse in the droop of his neck and slow swish of his tail. *Take care of him, boy.*

"He'll take fine care of your horse. Don't worry." She grabbed his elbow and tugged him toward the steps.

"Everyone's inside."

He stopped, pulling her to an awkward halt. Who else but his brothers and parents was she referring to? "Everyone?"

She grinned at him. "Mostly."

Come on, Silas, they won't bite. He reared back a bit when the thought popped into his mind. "Was that you?"

Yes. We are linked both emotionally and mentally. Surely you've noticed by now.

I suspected. He swallowed the nerves threatening to make him remount and ride away. Coming at her pleading request took every ounce of his courage. To face his parents again after their strained past. Who else would he confront? One of Cassie's frequent thoughts involved their dead ma. Facing the ghost of his mother seemed a daunting prospect. Still, if Cassie could, then so could he. He'd come this far. "Let's get it over with."

"You should know that all of us have some special ability, but we try to downplay them." She led him inside to a somewhat rustic entrance hall.

He examined the large space, noting a side door to the right leading to the covered span connecting the two structures, a swinging door at the back of the area peeking at a bustling kitchen, and off to the left a large arched door with tables and chairs occupied by a number of eating and talking guests. A long hallway stretched beyond the arched door into the new section to another side door leading outside. Nothing too fancy but it suited the region perfectly, much as he'd anticipated.

"It's a nice place to call home." He glanced toward the dining room when a pair of deep voices drew his attention.

The pair of men were large and burly, both with dark

hair and piercing eyes. The shorter of the two was far more powerful, with massive muscular arms and thighs. The other's easy, confident expression bespoke a man comfortable in his own skin. He peered closer, exploring the nuances of their expressions, their way of walking, and relaxed his guard. He needn't fear them just protect his private thoughts from their prying.

"There they are. Giles, Abram, look who's here." Cassie tugged Silas closer to the two large men approaching him.

"Hey, Silas, it's about time." Giles grabbed him into a bear hug.

The embrace felt like a literal bear had him until his oldest brother released him. "Damnation, man, when did you get so strong?"

A dark chuckle emerged from the other man's mouth. "A few months ago when our mother was murdered."

When she died, her binding spell broke and we got our powers back.

Silas glanced at Cassie, blinking rapidly at the message and the implications. "Binding spell?"

Abram peered closer at him and then glanced at Cassie. "You two can talk to each other without words?"

Cassie grinned. "Amazing, isn't it? It's a new power I've noticed as he's drawn closer. I could tell not only how he felt but sometimes knew what he was thinking."

Even though he had an inkling of the connection between them, Silas hadn't expected all his brothers also had special abilities. But as the reality settled in his conscious mind, he recalled glimpses from the past. When he and his brothers knew or could do things others could not. Once he left home, he no longer thought about any of those capabilities. As if they'd been erased from his memories. Until now.

"Ma did say you'd grow stronger with each of us coming home." Daniel sauntered into the hall to shake hands with Silas, his long strides bringing him quickly to a halt. Silas studied his next older brother, amazed at what a tall, strong, and good looking man he'd become. His intense green eyes, crinkling at the corners, bored into him for a moment then softened. "Welcome home."

Whoa. Not his home. He'd been traveling around the country and writing about what he found. He'd been doing so for so long that he didn't have a place to call home anywhere. He glanced around the entrance hall again, letting his senses absorb the emotions in the vicinity. The mixture of enjoyment and contentment from the guests bumped against the underlying anxieties of his brothers and sister as well as something more sinister. He concentrated on the sensation but couldn't pinpoint the source. Still, it didn't bode well for anyone. Perhaps he'd find a good story. Curiosity piqued, he intended to stay long enough to solve that mystery.

Silas nodded to Daniel. "Thanks. I'm glad to see you all looking so well."

"Did Cassie fill you in on everything?" Abram glanced at Cassie, waving a hand in the air as he turned back to meet Silas' gaze. "You know, using mind waves or whatever you use?"

"Not yet. Where's Ma?" The surprise on his brothers' faces made him smile. "Yes, I know that much. I'm not surprised because she was so irascible alive, why wouldn't she haunt the place?"

"Speaking of whom, look who decided to join us." Cassie motioned toward the front doors.

A shimmer blurred his view again until his mother's ghost appeared floating a few inches above the floor. She wore a long, blue dress and had her blond hair falling softly over her shoulders. She'd aged since he last laid eyes on her. She appeared harder, like life had dealt her a tough hand. Good. He blinked, unnerved despite knowing she haunted the inn.

Gathering his resolve close to his chest, he straightened his shoulders and nodded once. "Ma."

"Welcome, Silas." Mercy drifted closer to him, a tentative smile on her lips. "It's good to see you."

"Is it? Then why did you send me away?" The anger he'd suppressed for years burst from him before he could think better of expressing it. He wrestled it back under wraps but the outburst lingered in the air. The frantic, frightful days and nights he'd suffered when he'd left home. A boy really. He'd been fortunate to evade the worst of the men aiming to rob or hurt him. Then to meet the tavern owner who recognized his way with words and suggested he concentrate on a sound education. Reading and language consumed his life from then on.

"We had our reasons, son." She stretched a hand toward him as if to take one of his. "I can explain."

"Not here, please." Abram cast a worried glance around the hall. "The guests..."

"Good point." Giles motioned toward the dining room. "We don't need to stand out here. Come on into the dining room for some refreshments and we can quietly tell you what's been happening. You must be tired and thirsty after your journey."

"I'm used to riding long distances, but yeah, I'm tired." The blurry roof he'd thought he'd seen earlier demonstrated as much. "Got any ale?"

"Sure do." Daniel turned to lead the way into the dining room. "Follow me."

"I can't wait to introduce you to my fiancé, Flint Hamilton. He's been the innkeeper while Pa is away arranging for new furniture. And you'll want to meet our brothers' intended."

"Where'd Pa go?" Silas strode beside his sister as they entered the dining room, struggling to assimilate the flood of new information, both visually and by his overwhelmed senses, since his arrival. "But even more important, I can't wait to find out who would be daft enough to want to marry my brothers."

He skimmed his gaze over the room to take in its contents and get his bearings. To the right a mahogany bar gleamed in the lamplight, a display of colorful bottles of liquor against the wall behind it. A tall man rubbed the surface of the bar with a white cloth as he studied Silas for a long moment with clouded eyes. Ignoring the guarded look, he let his gaze roam the room. Some number of cloth-covered tables with six chairs around each arrayed throughout the room. An ornately carved and gleaming square piano occupied the front left corner of the room, with an empty blanket rack placed nearby. What was that there for? Cassie squeezed his arm to attract his attention and led him on inside.

"Pa went to Savannah, but he'll be home soon. He's on his way now with the furniture but also with others. Isaac, will you please get some refreshments for my brother, Silas Fairhope?"

The waiter crooked his left arm and draped a white towel over it. "Of course, Miss Fairhope. I'll return shortly."

"Thank you. Come on, Silas, over here." She stopped beside a table close to the bar. "Have a seat. There's so much to relay to you, Silas. We have much to discuss."

Good or bad? He settled onto the hard wooden chair she indicated, observing the play of emotions on her face and sensing the conflicting ones inside.

Yes.

He could only nod at her once, acknowledging the cautionary tone in her silent communication. What had he walked into by coming to this place in the middle of the wilderness?

Another brother had arrived. Flint suffocated the sigh struggling for release. Giles sauntered toward the bar, trying not to laugh. Well, Flint didn't find anything funny about the situation. Facing the inquisition of the newest stranger before he'd grudgingly grant his approval of the upcoming wedding of his sister. Flint rubbed the bar harder before realizing the futility of his action and snapped the towel up to hang it on the rail.

"I'll take an ale. What's the matter?" Giles slid onto the seat at the bar. "You look put out."

"Is that Silas?" Grabbing a mug, he filled it and set it in front of Cassie's oldest brother.

"Just arrived and already acting like he doesn't really want to be here." Giles took a swig of his drink then wiped the foam from his lips with the back of his hand. "Sounds familiar, doesn't it?"

"Indeed. I've been thinking about the sleeping arrangements with his arrival." Anything to divert his thoughts from the anticipated questions and searing looks of dismissal.

"Where do you want to put him?" Giles asked.

"In with you, and we can let Zander and Matt have the spare room." Flint had considered many other options but simply moving the two Simmons brothers in together so the Fairhope brothers could share seemed to make the most sense. "Does that suit you?"

Giles hefted his mug in a casual salute. "That's sensible. I'll introduce you to him, if you'd like."

"May as well." Flint braced his hands on the counter as Giles turned to beckon to his youngest brother.

The young man pushed his chair away from the table and strolled over to the bar. He resembled his brother Daniel most, having the same coloring and frame. Silas had curious blue eyes that assessed Flint with a quick sweep of his gaze. Flint could tell the other man was confident and easy going. A slow smile spread onto his mouth as he extended a hand toward Flint.

"Hello, you must be Flint Hamilton. I'm Silas Fairhope, Cassie's brother."

"Nice to make your acquaintance." Surprised by the easy familiarity, Flint accepted the man's firm grasp. "Was your journey pleasant?"

"Most of the time except for when I stumbled into a tavern in southern Kentucky where a band of highwaymen had also stopped for a rest." Silas raised his eyebrows and made a face. "Weary as I was, I didn't dare stay there. They'd have fleeced me but good. Old Traveler and I kept on down that particular road until we found a nicer spot."

"Your pretty face wouldn't be so pretty if you'd elected to linger." Giles tapped a fist on the bar. "Do you travel much?"

Silas nodded, a gleam in his eyes. "All the time. It's my job. I ride my sturdy Morgan all over the country, poking around to see what's what. Then I write up a piece and send it to the newspaper or magazine that hired me to write about a specific place."

"That's an interesting lifestyle you have." Traveling from place to place and then writing about the experience. Never staying in one place for very long. A wanderer of a sort. Intriguing. What must it be like to be in the saddle for days or weeks? Other than the obvious fatigue and sore muscles, Flint could envision the many interesting people he'd meet, the fine meals he'd enjoy in even finer establishments. Envy flashed through him. "Do you like it?"

"It has its moments, certainly." Silas pointed to the mug resting on the counter between Giles' hands. "Might I trouble you for one of those?"

"No trouble at all." Flint quickly filled another mug and slid it toward the newcomer. "Welcome to the inn. You can settle in with Giles, if that is all right with you."

"Bunk with my big brother? That's fine." Silas angled a grin at Giles. "I'll try to behave unlike when we were boys."

"You better." Giles tapped his fist on Silas' shoulder. "I can defend myself."

Rubbing his shoulder, Silas flashed a mock frown at him. "You're dangerous."

"Don't forget it." Giles lifted his mug and swallowed a long draught then let a sly smile ease onto his face. "It's my job."

Silas opened his mouth to reply but Flint waved him off. "Don't bother. He's the family Guardian and takes his role very seriously."

"Guardian of what exactly?" Silas asked, setting his mug

on the counter.

"Cassie will explain everything later. Not in the dining room." Flint glanced at Cassie where she waited at the table with her other brothers and their fiancés. Quite a group gathered in one place, each couple seated together around the table. He, too, belonged in that group, a thought which made him grin at Cassie. Silas' curious gaze reminded him of his manners. "You should meet the ladies, though, while you're in here. Giles, will you do the honors, please?"

"I'd be delighted." Giles stood and motioned for Silas to follow him.

A commotion at the back of the room drew Flint's gaze to where Allegro, the feisty blue-grey Merlin falcon, flew through the always open window to perch on Cassie's shoulder. Allegro's presence in the area was pure magic, as Merlins didn't stray far from the coast. But he'd come on his own to help Cassie anyway she needed. Her familiar came and went as the lightweight bird deemed necessary. Nobody but Cassie had any control or influence over the fast and intelligent creature.

Flint moved out from behind the bar to trail after the two men. Silas was not as hard to like as he'd feared. Indeed, he could see them being friends over time. His willingness to engage with others even though he didn't know them must be an asset while interviewing people from across the country. He halted at the table, standing behind Cassie's chair just out of reach of the falcon. To his credit, Silas barely flinched, almost as if he expected the bird's presence.

"You've met Flint, my betrothed." Cassie glanced up and back at Flint. "And this little guy on my shoulder is Allegro. I'll tell you more about him later. For now, I'll let

Giles introduce you to the rest."

Giles performed a half bow toward Silas. "Silas, I'd like for you to meet your future sisters. Abram's fiancé is Mandy Crawford, who works here in the dining room as the hostess."

Abram lifted Mandy's hand to hold, a possessive gesture if Flint ever saw one. The pair had literally run into each other after Abram first saw Mercy's ghost. He'd fled only to knock into the young woman. And knocking his senses aflutter over her enchanting person.

"Daniel has claimed Wilma Hamilton, Flint's sister, to be his bride." Giles waved a hand in their direction.

"It's amazing to me that I came here with the intention of staying only a pair of days but have fallen in love with this woman and this place." Daniel slowly shook his head, but he couldn't hide the delight in his expression.

"It's nice to meet you, Silas." Wilma smiled at the man as Daniel draped an arm around the back of her chair, his steady regard never flinching away. Wilma glanced at Daniel and then back to Silas. "I look forward to getting to know you, seeing as we'll be related before much longer."

Pride flooded Flint's chest as he regarded his sister. She'd become a fine young person, easy to look at, sure. With her auburn hair and dash of freckles across her nose, her fiery green eyes warning or welcoming depending on the situation. She presented a friendly façade, but she had a stubbornness she hid behind the acquiescing persona. Quietly stubborn described her attitude. She might say she agreed but she'd find a way to make her will known and obeyed in the end. But she was typically correct in her approach so he couldn't find fault with her. Plus she was superior with a bow and arrow, better than even their younger brother Julian.

Flint bit back a smile as Daniel exhibited yet another gesture of possession. These men obviously wanted to send the crystal-clear message their women were exactly that: theirs.

Giles glanced at Flint with humor twinkling in his eyes before returning his attention to Silas. "I'll introduce you to my fiancé later since Miss Baker is not here right now."

"You're engaged, too?" Silas widened his eyes as he slowly shook his head. "That's incredible."

"If you stay here long enough, you may have the same good fortune." Abram kissed the back of Mandy's hand and then leveled a serious look at Silas. "You are staying for a while, right?"

"Probably not. I have several people in other cities to meet with and take a tour of the must-see sights of their city." Silas pulled out a chair and sat down, resting his hands on his thighs. "I've allowed for a few days here, though."

Flint stared at the youngest brother in awe. He stated his fantastic lifestyle so casually. Once, Flint had dreamed of working in elegant hotels in one of the major cities. Meeting people from all walks of life. Exploring towns and historic sites alike. Perhaps building a fine hotel to attract the best of society. His gaze drifted around the mediocre dining room while the others continued their banter. Still much to do to raise the presentation to the standard he envisioned. But he'd stepped up its look considerably over the last few months.

How could he leave behind all the work he'd put into this inn? He shrugged inside. Mr. Fairhope might not require his assistance once he returned from his trip. Then where would Flint go? Back to his father's hotel in Huntsville most likely. He grimaced. Not a satisfactory situation any longer. Flint had worked on his own long enough now to want to continue in the same vein. He might have to convince Reggie to permit him to stay on as an assistant manager at least. But would that be enough? All his hard work and vision relegated to second place. His future loomed cloudy and unsatisfying.

"If you're only staying a short while, then we should talk soon." Cassie swept her gaze around the group and back to Silas. "Let's meet in the parlor after the supper rush is over. We can speak in private there."

Silas lifted one brow as he peered around the group's suddenly serious expressions. "Why not here and now?"

Flint laid a hand on the man's shoulder. " In private is safer. Trust me."

Chapter Two

Night had settled outside like a soft quilt over a sleeping baby. Cassie paced into the parlor ahead of her brothers, crossing the painted floor boards to stand by the conversation grouping near the snapping fireplace. The semicircle of cushioned armchairs with small tables interspersed had become the place for family discussions since Mercy's death. Odd how a tragedy could bring a family together. Silas closed the door behind him, then hesitated when his gaze landed on the immense doll's house between the front windows.

The inn had been her reluctant home for many years, or her virtual prison depending on her mood. Her ma had suppressed every idea, every desire, every dream she'd thought up. To the point that all Cassie wanted was to flee, to escape to freedom to do what she wanted. She'd started a side business of mending the guests' clothing in order to save up some money to make her desperate escape. Then Flint appeared, and she'd devised a new plan: marry him. Her ma would no longer have any say in her activities as a married woman. Little did she realize then that they'd actually fall in love and want to marry for real. The doll's house gave her a place to decorate as if she had her own home, a glimpse into a life yet realized.

Cassie sensed Silas' curiosity and confusion as he perused the house. "It was a birthday gift."

Silas lifted a brow at her as he strode closer to the two-story miniature house. "From?"

"Pa." She sighed at the memory of its arrival and the subsequent argument with her ma. "He sent it for my eighteenth birthday back in July."

Silas glanced at her. *It made you upset.*

I thought he'd sent it because he considered me still a child in need of playthings.

But?

She drew in a fortifying breath and let it out slowly. "Pa gave it to me so I could plan how I wanted to furnish my real-world home once I marry. But that's not what Ma led me to believe at the time."

Silas squatted down to peer inside the hinged open side of the house. "You've done a nice job with the tiny furniture and rugs and such."

Cassie rested a hand on the roof with growing pride while her brother inspected the interior. "Thank you." She slid her hand across the tiny shingles to check a loose tile near the chimney poking through the top of the house. "It's been a relaxing thing to work on when I have a few minutes now and then."

She laid her hand on the roof at the base of the chimney as Silas shifted to look into the dining room on the first floor. Suddenly her hand warmed and she looked closer at the rooftop. An image appeared in her mind's eye: red, yellow, and blue flames licking up the side of the house, hungrily devouring the building. The heat and terrible sight shook her to the core. Shock and grief flashed through her chest. With a small cry, she jerked her hand away from the doll's house and Silas leapt to his feet, concern etched into his features.

"What?"

"It was on fire." She rubbed her hand until it cooled to normal, replaying the scary scene in her mind. "I don't understand."

Mercy shimmered into view beside Silas. "What don't you understand?"

"Oh! Ma, I thought you were going to stop popping in like that." Cassie drew a shaky breath, startled and upset combined. "What perfectly abysmal timing."

"I'm sorry. I didn't think." Mercy shrugged lightly but the gleam in her eyes belied her apology.

"You might have scared Silas." Cassie peered at him but sensed only mild surprise. No fear or concern at the sudden appearance of their ma's haint. *You're not upset at all, are you?*

I have known for some time that she haunted the place. Silas winked at her and then leveled his gaze on Mercy. "Hello, mother."

"I'm glad to see you again, son." Mercy floated above the floor, drifting closer to him. "I see you've discovered your innate gift, your ability to speak silently with others."

"Indeed. I noticed it a few months ago, over the summer." He inspected Mercy's semi-translucent figure. "How did it happen?"

"My death?" Mercy shimmered, her agitation apparent in the trembling of her pale-blue dress. "I was shot in the head. In my own bedroom."

"Shot?" Silas angled his shocked gaze at Cassie. "What on earth happened?"

"Some men thought she had valuables up there and when she didn't, they killed her." My how she hated relaying the truth. Reviving the wave of guilt at her careless slip of tongue which led to her mother's awful end. "Flint insists it wasn't my fault but I still think it wouldn't have happened if not for me."

If only she hadn't said in front of strangers that her ma had supposed treasures in her room. Trinkets more like it, but the men took her at her word and her ma paid the price. How could she ever forgive herself? She'd learned a valuable lesson from the experience and the subsequent guilt: keep her mouth shut about their private business.

Giles crossed his arms over his chest. "Flint's right, Cassie. You didn't pull the trigger. You're not responsible for those men's actions."

"I know, but they wouldn't have formed the plan to rob her if I hadn't given them the idea there was something worth stealing." She splayed her hands and spun toward her mother's ghost. If only she could hug her ma, feel her comforting arms around her. "I am sorry."

"I agree with Flint and Giles, dear. It's not your fault in the slightest." Her ma drifted closer, holding out her arms as she solidified. "Come here."

Cassie blinked, surprise washing through her. She'd forgotten her ma could materialize for brief moments. She stepped into the embrace but as her ma's arms wrapped around her, they dissolved into soft cloud-like arms that passed through her. Tears sprang to Cassie's eyes as she stepped back, disappointed.

"I can't seem to maintain a solid form very long

anymore." Mercy frowned as she shook her head. "I don't understand what's happening to me."

"Which reminds me, Cassie, what happened when you touched the roof?" Abram crossed his ankles as he leaned back in his chair beside the fireplace.

She'd suppressed the vision but the reminder brought it vividly back. The hot flames. The smell of burning wood. Fear. "I saw it burning, fully aflame. I've never had visions before." She peered at her ma, sensing and seeing an awareness of something inside her. "What's happened to me?"

"I believe you've developed foresight." Mercy glanced at Silas and then nodded once before returning her gaze to Cassie. "As I thought, with the coming of each of your brothers, your combined powers are growing. You're stronger together than separated. The reason we sent you all apart before my father discovered how strong you would be."

"So now she can see future events? That's useful." Daniel leaned forward in his seat, grinning at her. "Tell me my future, Cassie."

"You don't have one if you keep joking with me." Cassie shook her head at him as she returned his grin. Then she met her mother's pleased expression. "You seem right happy today, Ma."

"I am happy to see all my children together and getting along fine." She folded her hands in front of her. "If only Reggie were here to see this."

"He's on his way." Giles rested his hands on his knees. "He said he'd be here by Allhallows which is only a couple weeks from now."

"I wish I could stay that long." Silas sighed as he moved

to sit in a vacant chair facing the doll's house. "But I have responsibilities elsewhere and many people waiting to talk to me."

"You can't leave until Pa gets home. We have a witch hunter stalking about." Cassie crossed to stand in front of Silas, sensing his desire to keep his visit short, to move on as he was wont to do. "I understand you usually flit about, but we also have our aunts trying to persuade me to join their efforts with dark magic. Together we're stronger, so now we can defeat both threats, or at least hold them at bay until Pa deals with them."

Resistance and reluctance flooded Silas as he studied her for several moments. *Talking silently isn't much of a weapon, sis.* "I doubt I can be of much help."

"I bet you're really good with words, aren't you?" Mercy shifted side to side for a moment.

"I'm a writer, yes." Silas peered at her with puzzlement plain on his face. "So?"

"You're inherently able to manipulate the language, to weave spells with specifically chosen words." Mercy pointed at him with one ghostly finger. "You, my dear son, are a spellcaster."

Cassie clapped her hands together with glee. "Perfect. You can help me with my lame spells."

Silas pushed to sit upright and gripped the arms of the chair. "Are you telling me my ability to write acceptable articles is because I'm a witch?"

"Warlock, but yes." Mercy nodded as she drifted a foot away from him. "Even as a boy, your gift was apparent to any of us able to see it for its reality."

"Which again explains why you bound all of our powers." Abram nodded sagely, eyes glittering. "You couldn't have our secrets get out."

Silas pivoted his head to stare up at his mother. "You bound our powers? So you're a witch, too?"

She half-shrugged and pursed her lips. "We had to, you know. To keep you all safe."

Cassie laid a hand on Silas' tense arm. "When she died, her spell was broken. That's when all the family secrets started leaking out. Did you know Pa has a family full of witches and warlocks as well? Some of them may even be making the journey from Savannah with him."

"Let me try to grasp what you're telling me." *It's a lot to absorb in one sitting.* He rubbed a hand over his head, pulling his hair out of the queue to hang on his shoulders. "Ma's sisters and father are witches and warlocks, and Pa's, too. And we weren't told any of this growing up. Sent away from home once we reached our teen years to fend for ourselves. All to keep our magical origins a secret from our grandfather?"

Giles stood and shrugged. "In a nutshell, yes."

"Welcome home, brother." Daniel tapped the armrest as he grinned at the group at large. "It's about time."

"Nope, that's your gift." Abram chuckled, making a rolling motion with his right hand. "Time skipping and bouncing, I mean."

"Speaking of time, it's time for me to get back to work." Cassie surveyed the happy expressions of her brothers and even her mother. "Tomorrow we'll need to make a plan but for now, let's call it a night, shall we?"

"Just one more thing, Silas." Mercy glided closer to him, her expression sober. "We should talk about how to use your gift most effectively."

"Spellcasting?" Silas studied her, eyes wide. "It's simply

writing words, isn't it?"

Cassie could barely detect her brother's simmering confusion and resistance to all the revelations he'd been subjected to over the past few hours. Over time acceptance may replace the resistance if only at a slow rate.

"It's far more than that. Let's meet in my attic tomorrow morning and I'll explain." Mercy shimmered as Silas acknowledged her request with a dip of his head. "Good night."

She disappeared and Cassie let out the air in her chest. "Are you all right?"

Silas nodded and then stood. "It's been quite a day. I think I'll retire for the evening."

"Sleep well." She watched as he snared his ribbon from the arm of the chair and strode purposefully across the floor to the stairs up to where he'd stay with Giles. *Don't worry. It will all look different in the morning.*

After Silas broke his fast the next morning, he ambled up the stairs and halted outside his parents' bedroom door. He jingled the keyring Cassie had placed in his hand at the dining room table, her silent reassurance anything but reassuring. The more he contemplated what he might face on the other side of the door, let alone up in the attic, the more he quaked in his scuffed leather boots. His sister's calm acceptance of her witchy ways unfortunately hadn't transferred into him. Yet.

Mercy appeared at his side with a flash of white light, making him jump sideways.

"Ma!"

She chuckled and motioned for him to proceed. "Go on

in. There's nothing inside to hurt you. I'll meet you up in the attic." Then she disappeared, leaving him to stare at the closed door.

He sucked in a fortifying breath and lifted the latch. Keeping his eyes on the spiral staircase, he climbed up to the locked door. Which key was it? He fumbled through the set until he found the one Cassie had pointed out to him. Soon the door stood open into the dimly lit room. He shuddered with dread. A darkened room brought back too many bad memories. Memories of isolation and loneliness. Nights spent dreading the advent of a new day when he'd face more challenges and terrors. He hurried to the oil lamp on a small table by the window, lifted the fire starter and soon had the wick burning. The lamplight chased the shadows away as Silas slowly surveyed the room's contents, easing his held breath out in stages.

The cozy space exuded a sense of serenity and mystery. A cream-colored blanket draped over the back of the chair by the table, waiting for his mother to occupy. A cold Franklin stove enjoyed a central position in the room. Obviously, his mother spent much time in the confines of the small room hidden away at the top of the house.

One wall featured shelves and shelves of leather- and cloth-bound books. He walked over to read the titles on the spines. Books about various kinds of magic, of spells, of using runes. Instructions for using the necessary implements of witchcraft. Three on identifying poisonous plants and how to use them most effectively. A chill swept through him at the idea of his mother employing any of those.

He turned to survey the rest of the room. Several trunks stood arrayed around the space. A large, flat-top trunk was near the door, its front wall bedecked with carved flowers and arches. A slightly smaller wood one was lighter in color with carved flowers and arches, a flat top displaying scratches and rings that looked like they'd been made from a sweating glass. Another trunk made from pale wood, with a domed lid and a scroll-like design plus the same flying owl as on the door key, rested to one side.

"There you are." Mercy popped into view over by the trunks. She drifted from one to the other, finally stopping at the edge of the floral rug covering the center of the floor to gaze at him. "Are you ready to begin?

He placed the fire starter on the table and wiped his hands on his dark blue trousers. "I suppose you have something you believe I should know."

"Very perceptive of you." Mercy shook her head. "And sarcastic, but I'll not harp upon your attitude for the moment."

"Thank you, mother." He really couldn't stop the scorn in his tone. Bitterness from his forced expulsion from his boyhood home seared the back of his throat. "What did you wish to convey to me?"

She crossed her arms over her chest, her long blue dress floating around her hovering feet as if a breeze flowed through the still room. "The very first thing you need to know, my dear son, is to let everything go."

"What's that supposed to mean?" He had little enough to call his own. Was she suggesting he dispose of the few things he possessed? To what end? "I only have what I need to survive on the road, Ma. What would you have me to do?"

"Not your belongings. In order to conjure with your magic, you must let go of everything inside of you that is tame." She drifted a few feet closer, her aqua-blue eyes glittering in the lamplight. "Open yourself to the sound of the world around you, the opportunities that nature shares with us."

"I-I don't understand." How could nature be part of his actions, his goals, his desires?

"My son, you've traveled the country. Where is your wonder at what you saw? What you experienced?" She flung her arms out to her sides, whirling in place. "The world of creation is a secret place open only to the creator. You must let go of any preconceived ideas in order to let your creations be free."

He studied her in silence for a long moment. "You speak from experience?"

"Indeed." She pointed to the carpet at her feet. "Roll that up out of the way and I'll teach you everything you need to know in order to come into your spellcrafting powers. The power you possess inside has not fully been tapped by your writing so far. But with a little encouragement and guidance, you'll realize your full potential as a writer and as a warlock."

He bent to roll the carpet out of the way, amazed at the drawing on the floorboards hidden by the rug. Dusting his hands off, he perused the symbols exposed to the flickering light. Without knowing what they meant, he surmised the shapes and colors had specific meanings. Oriented around a large circumscribed circle, they probably aligned with the ordinal directions of a compass as well. He peered at his mother, aware of the knowing gleam in her ghostly eyes.

"Very good. You have an innate affinity with the sacred circle elements."

"Sacred circle, hm?" He strolled around the circle, trying to interpret the symbols' meanings. "You'll need to enlighten me about their meaning, but I think I do have a fundamental understanding of the significance of them."

"You have much to learn about the symbols, the God and Goddess, and the accoutrements of our magic." She shifted from side to side and then paused. "But first, let us speak of the spells you will want to craft. Of how to choose the right words to create the effect, the result if you will, that you intend."

"So it comes down to word choice, does it?" He crossed his arms and braced his feet apart to regard his mother. "That is far from surprising."

"Sometimes we intend one thing but say another and the results can be catastrophic." She turned away, drifting to stare out the closed window above the table where the lamp burned.

"Again, you appear to be speaking from experience." He dropped his arms and walked toward her. "What happened?"

"Our family has endured much heartache and I do not wish to relive it." Mercy spun to face him, her eyes clouded with remembered sorrow. "That's not why we're here."

"I'm here, at this inn, because Cassie wrote to me to come and help her after your death. While I knew before I arrived that I'd find you haunting the inn, I didn't know there'd be so many secrets and problems to be confronted and overcome. Now I want to know, to understand the past." What other surprises were in store for him the longer he remained? Steeling himself, he shrugged at his mother. "I have no idea what happened to make you and Pa flee here to this wilderness so far from the rest of your family. Nor do I know why Pa kept his family away, hidden from us. Why don't you start there?"

"We had such a lovely place in Montgomery. I so wish we hadn't been forced to abandon it." She slowly shook her head as her eyes turned inward, remembering better days. "The big manor house surrounded by flowering and fruit trees. We lived close to my sisters and my parents when we were first married, so gathered together frequently. But something changed and my sisters began to pressure me in uncomfortable ways. Wanting me to help them with dark magic. I couldn't. It went against everything our mother had taught us about being good witches and helping others to have love and joy in their lives."

"I remember having dinners with the family when I was a boy, but that suddenly changed." He tapped a finger against his chin, trying to jostle the memory loose. His cousin's drowning. That was it. "After George died?"

"It started then. We had to do what me must to protect you all. That put a definite strain on the family ties. But the final break happened when my sisters blamed me for our mother's death six years later." Mercy hugged her waist as she frowned at him. "I didn't kill her, no matter what they claim. They gave me the wrong amounts of the ingredients of a potion, which caused the cauldron to explode while I was out gathering more of a hard-to-find plant."

"Sounds like it was an accident, not intentional." What had happened between his cousin's death and his grandmother's, though, that increased the tension within the family? He suspected there was more to the story than what his mother had willingly relayed.

"Possibly, but why would they tell me the wrong thing? I think our father put them up to it but I have no proof of that. Only my conviction as to his goals and using my gullible sisters to achieve them." Mercy's translucent shoulders rocked before she quelled the shiver by tightening her grip on her waist. "Everything we did, we did to keep you and your brothers, and Cassie of course, safe from the diabolical deeds of my father and then my sisters. I couldn't stop them, but I could protect you all. Which is what we did by binding your powers and moving away."

"But you kept Cassie with you. From what I gather, you didn't care as much about me and my brothers, just kicked us out on our own. But her? You kept her close. Why?"

Anguish and fear swept through Silas from his mother's ghostly form. He shielded himself from the onslaught of emotion as he braced for her answer.

"We loved you all. You must believe me." She worried her lower lip and then sighed. "But Cassie's the key to everything. We had to keep her away from them no matter the cost to the rest of us."

Chapter Three

Silas needed air so he'd grabbed his hat and headed out to explore the Fury Falls Inn property. Ambled up the hill away from the inn and his family to seek out the famous falls and healing springs for himself. Silas hadn't anticipated any of the revelations dumped on his head and his heart over the last twenty-four hours. A man needed some warning to set up some kind of defense. Cassie could have warned him before he'd arrived but she hadn't. Well, he had detected her concern ratcheting up. But never in his wildest moments would he have conjured such disclosures about his family. The history of who they were, let alone what they'd done, accused each other of, and then the resulting punishments toward each other. Binding powers. Banning children from home. Disappearing into the northern wilderness of the state to hide. All because of what? A misunderstanding? A miscalculation? The journalist in him craved answers. But at the moment, he still reeled from everything he'd learned in such a short amount of time.

He paused to lift his hat and swipe a hand over his

brow, the slight climb bringing a dew of sweat from the exertion. The view from the trail stunned him. He hadn't expected the foothills of the mountains to be so beautifully dressed in fall colors. Hadn't thought through what he might find upon his arrival at the inn. Crimson, red, gold, and pale yellow intermixed and seamed together with the dark green of the evergreen trees. The combination soothed the agitation in his gut. He breathed in the scent of the fallen tree leaves scattered and crushed underfoot along with the aroma of the pine needles. The rush and splash of the nearby creek played against the cry of a hawk above. Nature. His mother's words echoed in his brain. About nature and wonder and creating magic. With new appreciation, he scanned his surroundings, opening his mind and soul to the world around him.

"Hey, Silas, what brings you up here?" Giles strode down the hill toward him, his wide-brimmed hat shading his eyes from the morning sun. "I thought you were working with Ma."

"I was but we're done for the day." He couldn't stay and absorb any more about magic or the family's past. Didn't want to hear how the sisters fought. Or excuses for why his parents scattered them to the four winds. "Why are you up here?"

"Walking the property, making sure it's secure as much as possible." Giles propped his hands on his hips, his restless gaze roaming the surrounding woods. "Just keeping an eye on things."

"Guardian duties, huh?" Silas nodded as he drank in the peace and quiet of the area. Such a lovely place, one inviting and welcoming at the same time. "How long you staying?"

"Forever, I think." Giles chuckled, seeing Silas' bemused expression. "I plan to build a house down the lane a piece. A place where Haley and I can live and raise a family."

"Are you tired of living on the road, is that why?" On dark nights in a strange bed, Silas pondered how long he'd be moving from place to place, adventure to adventure, interview to interview. When would he find the right place to settle down and call it home? When would he want to do so? The very idea made him want to take a ride on his horse. "I think that's the only reason to build a house."

"I haven't done all that much traveling. After I left home, I went to Mobile and found work on the docks before I ultimately started my own importation and exportation business."

"You started on the docks? That's a rough place to work, isn't it?" Silas had little experience along the coast but the few times he'd ventured onto the docks after a story he'd quickly learned to steer clear of certain sailors and shoremen. Their lives involved a great deal of defending themselves and their work any way possible, usually with fists and other weapons.

"Every day, but it taught me a great deal, including how to fight for what I believe in." Giles shoved one hand into a pocket. "Now I believe in our family and defending it and everyone associated with us. I can't do that if I leave, now can I?"

His oldest brother had always looked out for others. For him to give up his own business to ensure the health and welfare of the family proved how loyal he still remained despite all that transpired since being pushed out of the nest. Yet accepting the amount of upheaval his choice entailed surprised Silas. He couldn't simply change who he was to suit his family.

"Speaking of your Guardian role, Ma just told me something shocking to me." He still had a hard time assimilating the concept. "It's about Cassandra."

"There is much about Cassie that can be quite surprising." Giles smirked at Silas and then tilted his head. "What is it?"

"That she's the 'key to everything' although she didn't elaborate." Silas heard a bird cry above and glanced to the sky in time to see a falcon dart across the gray clouds building above. Rain moving in. He lowered his gaze to peer at Giles. "Any idea what she meant by that?"

"I'm afraid so. Come on. I need to get back to her." Giles started walking down the trail, leaving Silas gaping after him for a beat.

"I'm coming." Silas jogged to catch up to his brother, falling into step as they marched down the path toward the stable and inn. "I'm confused, too."

Giles stayed focused on the trail as he increased his pace. "She has the most power among us and thus we need to protect her from the manipulations of our aunts and the deadly intent of the witch hunter. Then and only then will she come into her full power and our family will be safe. Without her, that won't happen and the family will break apart forever."

Silas stumbled over an invisible obstacle on the path, catching his balance with a jig of steps. "Oh, is that all."

Flint carried a broom to the front porch to sweep away the dirt and leaves gathering around the chairs and tables spaced along its length. The building clouds cast light shadows on the stone drive. A lazy Sunday morning, the scent of rain bringing a sense of much needed peace along with it. The horses nickered occasionally, the cattle mooing in their field, the hogs rooting around the edges of the forest. A few customers greeted him on their way inside for breakfast, clomping up the steps and on through the doors. He energetically employed the straw broom, glad for a few minutes outside the confines of the building. The sound of horse hooves drew his gaze to the lane leading up to the inn. He smiled at the approach of the deputy, his new friend, on his fine horse.

"Hail and greetings, Flint." The burly man reined his horse to a halt at the hitching rail and swung from the creaking leather saddle to drop with a thud on the stone carriageway. "How fare you on this fine morning?"

"I'm well. And you?" Flint leaned the broom against the front wall and then crossed to meet Barney Parker at the top of the steps. "I wasn't expecting you."

"I'm doing fine as well." He motioned to the new addition, the fresh wood softly gleaming in the morning light. "You've added on to the inn, I see. Business must be good."

"More and more people venture out to enjoy the springs as well as sample the fine meals." Flint's efforts to improve the services at the roadside inn had been accepted eagerly by the growing populace of the state. A state only shy of its two-year anniversary of statehood by two months, in fact. Yet more and more residents arrived with fair weather to enjoy the lush and prosperous area. Perhaps he should start planning some kind of special event to commemorate the statehood anniversary. He'd talk to Cassie about it. More pressing was the reason for his friend's unexpected appearance. "What brings you out today?"

"I have news but I wanted to see how things were going here." He glanced about at the people coming and going on horseback, in wagons, emerging from coaches and carriages. "Like you said, obviously people enjoy coming here."

"There you are." Cassie let the door close behind her as she came toward Flint. "I've been looking everywhere for you."

"I'm right here. Give me a moment." Flint took hold of Cassie's hand to keep her close as he sought an answer to his question for Barney. "What news do you have?"

Barney removed his hat and held it at his side. "Morning, Miss Fairhope. I'm glad you're here as this concerns you as well." He cleared his throat and sighed. "The man found guilty for your mother's death was hanged yesterday."

"Oh my." Cassie pressed her free hand to the base of her throat.

Flint squeezed her hand, understanding the news upset her. "Well deserved, too. What of the others?"

He'd kept his own counsel on the fates of the three men responsible for the attack and death of Mercy. Young Teddy's father, Adam, along with another man, Joe, had been kept in jail until Greg's hanging. Flint hadn't mentioned anything to Cassie about the date of the execution knowing she'd worry over it for no good reason. While the death of a good man would upset many, not so for murderers and criminals. He told Giles as the family's Guardian and they'd decided to not mention it to anyone else. Nobody could change the eventuality and they didn't need to witness the event. Better for everyone's sake to be spared the possible distress of the experience.

"They've been released for time served in their role as accomplices." Barney shifted to hold his hat in front of him. "They didn't kill anyone, only conspired to rob. And they didn't steal anything of real value, just that set of keys."

The keys in question were more valuable than they'd let on. They unlocked Mercy's private attic where the family's magical heirlooms remained in trunks and on the shelves. He'd only been permitted in the attic a couple of times, the Fairhopes choosing to keep the contents of the room their private business. Which didn't stop him wondering what else might be kept under lock and key away from prying eyes.

"So Adam is free to come here and take Teddy home with him?" Cassie turned fearful eyes to Flint. "He'd interrupt the boy's education, as meager as it is under my tutelage, if he does so. The boy will be devastated."

Barney rotated his hat slowly between his hands. "He is the boy's father, so he has that right."

Not on Flint's watch. He'd grown quite attached to the lad. The boy had the opportunity to make something more of himself than a criminal's servant. The man abandoned the boy while he was off causing trouble and wreaking havoc. Getting involved with the low-life likes of Greg to steal and kill instead of teaching his son how to be a real man. An honest and upstanding citizen of the community. Ha. Adam didn't know how to be one himself so he couldn't teach his son anything worthwhile.

"Just another concern to manage." Cassie folded her arms and sighed.

"Anything I should know about?" Barney glanced at her and then Flint. "More troubles?"

Flint squared his shoulders. Troubles? Like the feeling of being watched? The aunts wanting to cause their own kind of mischief with regards to his fiancé? The murders of witches living alone that seemed to occur closer and closer to the inn until he feared for Cassie's life? Those troubles? But he couldn't share them with his friend, with law enforcement, without Giles there to back him up. Or without Giles knowing and agreeing to the disclosure. Flint shared a silent quelling look with Cassie before he replied.

"I don't think there's anything to share at the moment." True as far as it went. He wouldn't lie outright, just maybe by omission in this case. In the meantime, he wanted to make it up to his friend somehow. He patted the flintlock pistol at his side. "Say, Barney, would you want to do a little target practice later? I haven't had any reason to fire my weapon and I want to make sure I'm sharp."

Barney arched a dark brow at the suggestion. "I see. Sure, I'm willing to sharpen your aim if that will make you feel better. But I have a couple things I need to take care of this morning. Mid-afternoon at the cave?"

"Sounds fine to me."

"I hope it's a waste of time and you never need to use that gun, Flint." Cassie scrutinized him until he wanted to squirm but resisted. Then she addressed Barney with a sincere smile. "Deputy, might you and the sheriff be interested in attending our open house and celebration of Allhallows this year?"

"That's a fine idea, Cassie." Flint nodded at his friend.

"I love a good party, so of course. I'll let Sheriff Neal know, too." Barney replaced his hat on his head with a tap on the crown. "I'm off for now, but I'll see you later, Flint."

"Until then." Flint watched the deputy trot down the

steps and mount his horse with easy grace. The man once had seemed to have a grudging attitude toward him, but he'd changed as Flint came to know him better. They trusted each other. They did. His heart sank. He really should tell him the truth of their situation and their fears. But how could he?

Chapter Four

*C*assie hovered her hands over the keyboard of the polished square piano and met Giles' wary eyes. She lifted the corners of her mouth into an encouraging smile and started playing the song they'd rehearsed. "When life seems hard and oh so wrong..."

The chatter of the dozens of customers in the room quieted as the first strains filled the air. Giles strummed his guitar, adding harmony to the main melody Cassie played. She'd specifically chosen her calming songspell in order to help Giles relax as well as to see if the combination of their instruments created any difference in how the audience reacted to the music.

She surveyed the people in the room, reaching out with her senses to ascertain their mood and response. "Soft, soft be still and calm..."

Mandy performed her role as hostess, moving through the room in her pristine white blouse and long, dark blue skirt, stopping to chat with the guests. She elicited smiles and nods with her inquiries, so Cassie assumed the guests must be enjoying the meal and hopefully the entertainment.

Her friend had slipped into her new role with ease, much happier working with the customers than with food in the kitchen. Flint still needed to find a couple more kitchen maids to help out Matt with the preparation of the array of dishes necessary to feed so many customers. Meg and Myrtle Marple, the sisters who'd worked in the kitchen for years now, couldn't possibly keep working as hard as they must be for an extended period. Perhaps Cassie should talk to Flint about finding more help and soon.

Flint hustled behind the bar to fill the drink orders from the two waiters, Larry and Isaac. She couldn't wait to be able to call him her husband. Tall, handsome, loving, kind, and right now she sensed his worry and anxiety. She concentrated on him more, infusing her voice with love and peace aimed his direction. His anxiety lessened but lingered as Larry carried a tray of drinks over to the group of men she thought of as the gang at the back of the room. The group numbered close to fifteen, growing from a handful to double digits over the last month. Among them, esteemed banker Sterling Nelson sat at one end of the pushed together tables, with an empty chair next to him. Probably for John Baker, her pa's friend and the man tasked to supervise Flint's efforts, if she had to guess. Those two seemed to be together more and more and she didn't like it. Not one bit. She had to work with him and the uncertainty of what he might be doing on the sly worried her. What were they scheming about in her father's dining room?

Allegro darted through the open window near the gang and then swooped toward Cassie, alighting on his perch nearby. The falcon's presence calmed her own agitation as Aunt Hope and Aunt Faith swept into the dining room from the entrance hall, their long ebony skirts swishing about their shoes, to flounce onto their preferred seats near the piano. Faith's cat, her devious familiar, stalked into the room and leapt onto an empty seat. Faith shot a glare at Hope and then aimed her hate-filled eyes at Cassie before blinking once. Had the sisters argued? She filled her voice with more calm and acceptance. But all three of them stared at her. Glared at her with narrowed eyes. Again. She stifled the aggravated sigh threatening to interrupt the song. With a lift of her head, she signaled to Giles to repeat the chorus so she could try to calm her aunts' suspicious regard. Though she doubted anything she sang could do so. Silas strode into the room, pausing at the arched doorway to peer at Cassie.

What's wrong, sis? I could sense your distress from outside.

Our aunts just won't give up their attempt to sway me to them.

His gaze landed on the pair of witches. *Let me see what I can do.*

Good luck, you'll need it!

Silas went to claim a seat at the same table as Hope and Faith, a pleasant smile pasted on his lips as he sat down with them. They seemed pleased by his attention and willingness to engage in conversation. Perhaps he'd have some influence after all. His way with words likely applied to his discourse with others.

A movement at the doorway drew her attention. John Baker strode into the dining room with a possessive air about him, acting as if he owned the place which was far from the truth. He nodded at her in greeting but hurried to the back of the room to join the gang. Taking the empty chair next to Sterling as she'd predicted. He exuded confidence but also a hint of restraint as he entered into the ongoing conversation among the men. None of them were the upstanding citizens they portrayed themselves to be. Or they wouldn't confer and connive together. John flagged down Larry who hurried over to the table, efficiently taking the gang's orders for refreshments. Mr. Baker remained a contradiction in her soul, both polite to her and in cahoots with the gang they suspected were responsible for the murders. Her pa trusted him, but could she? Should she?

She finished the spellsong with a flourish, and then rose to take a bow along with Giles as the guests applauded. A first in a long while. They really seemed to respond more enthusiastically with the two of them playing. She smiled her thanks at them and then turned to address her brother. "Thank you, Giles. That was a lot of fun. We should play together more often."

"Surprisingly, I enjoyed that as well." Giles shrugged. "I didn't expect to but they all seemed to like it."

"And I think that Ma's 'stronger together' claim works for my music, or rather our music, as well."

"That's an interesting thought, Cassie." Giles cradled his guitar against his waist. "And a good reason for us to stay together as much as possible. I aim to keep you close so I can keep you safe."

She'd agreed to another guard because at least Giles actually was her intended Guardian. Teddy had tried, of course, sitting with her while she worked in the garden or read in the gazebo. But he was a mere boy. She enjoyed his company, and wanted to do all she could as his stand-in teacher until other arrangements could be made, but a guard he was not. She sensed a growing danger at the inn, one she wasn't sure she could counter even with all her magic. She nodded to her brother, glad of the offer.

"I like having you nearby." She laid her hand on his steely arm. "I feel safer to be honest. Thank you."

"You're welcome. How about some cider after all your singing?" He set his guitar down by the piano, and proffered his arm.

She accepted his offer and they walked toward the bar. Suddenly, she sensed a swelling undercurrent of acceptance, subtle and nearly undetectable. Like someone nudged the entire roomful of people to be open and willing to accept...what? She blinked as she surveyed the room, seeking the source but to no avail. In fact, the nudge didn't seem to be from any of the witches in the room. She reached out to Silas.

Do you feel that?

What?

That...nudge?

Maybe. Can you describe it more?

Never mind. It's ephemeral and now it's gone.

Perhaps it was her imagination. The longer she thought about it the more convinced she became of the sensation she'd felt. Despite its coming and going, she'd swear she'd sensed someone trying to influence the room at large. But who? And why? She'd keep her eyes and senses open, searching for the answers.

I can no longer merely observe this growing coven of witches right beneath my nose. That Fairhope girl is the center of the activity, always flaunting her magic. She must be the keystone of the group or those other witches and warlocks wouldn't be observing her so closely. They need her for some inexplicable reason but they are all a threat.

Even her bird is a menace to the entire community. She has to go before the rest can be stopped. And I know the right man who can take care of the chit.

I lifted a finger to snare his attention. "I have a little something I need you to do."

The waiter paused in listening to the silly refreshment orders to peer at me. He moved around the table to stand close by and leaned down. "Yes, sir?"

"It's time to remove the leader of the coven, Cassandra Fairhope. I don't need to know how you do it, but let me know when it's done. Understood?"

"Yes, sir."

The temperature in the dining room shifted from warm to cool to frosty in as many beats of Silas' heart. Then warmed again. Silas tried to listen to his aunts but his senses quivered with the varying emotional states in the room. Someone was influencing a changing group of people but not with magic. Something else was at work.

"I was unaware you felt neglected, sister." Hope studied Faith with a haughty frown on her brow. "I value your assistance and advice."

Faith lifted her chin. "You do not always make it obvious."

Hope inclined her head for a moment before shifting in her chair to face Faith. "I will try to do better in future. I suppose I've been concerned with our need to convince Cassandra of her destiny, of her purpose in life."

The last statement caught Silas' attention, dragging it away from his perusal of the people in the dining room. "Her purpose?"

Faith lifted a brow as she gazed at him. "Our father knew she would one day take our sister's place in the trinity. After she matured, of course. Given Mercy made it clear of her refusal. That Cassandra would be an even greater asset toward furthering our aims. But the chit has denied us."

"We simply must have her consent and her willing participation to craft the strongest magic. That is why we frequent this table, to remind her of her duty to the family. To prompt her to reconsider her foolish refusal." Hope slowly shook her head. "There's no other path forward."

Silas stared at his aunts, contemplating their reason for sitting at the table day in and day out. Stalking his sister in the vain hope of turning her to their side. He'd only been at the inn a couple ofe days but he could tell his aunts wouldn't succeed. Cassie's stubborn streak shone brightly. Even when a child, she'd exhibited determination to follow through with her desires no matter what obstacles arose to deter or thwart them. Mandy sashayed past his table, a small smile on her lips. She met his studious gaze and then he knew.

She was the source of the nudge Cassie mentioned. She didn't employ magic, but she used her welcoming smile and soft voice to help the guests feel part of the inn's story. That their presence and their business created a place of acceptance and a second home for them. As such, the customers shared in the continuing success of the business but also of the family. No matter which kind of creature they might be. They were all family.

Mandy's need to be accepted pulsated through her. He sensed it as the strongest emotion in the room. A warm glow inside her as the guests returned her smile, or said kind words about the place, about the food, about her as hostess. Like she played the part of matriarch of the inn in one sense. Overseeing everyone's happiness, satisfaction, but mostly that they were welcomed into the flock.

Her smile had included him, welcomed him into the family. How satisfying it felt to feel like he belonged after wandering the countryside for years on his own. Adrift like the leaves falling from the trees outside. Without a firm direction, or plan, or even destination, but always on the move with the merest breath of wind. At that moment, everyone around him exuded contentment. Was that the work of Cassie's songspell or of Mandy's subtle efforts? Or perhaps the combination of both magic and matriarch?

Opening his soul to both nature and its inherent mystical properties, to the natural magic flowing through every plant, animal, and human. The amazing possibilities of that combination could make some very potent potions.

I discovered the source of the nudge you felt. It's nothing to worry about.

Are you sure?

Yes. Trust me.

Cassie nodded at him from the bar where she stood between Giles and Flint, sipping on a mug of cider. *I do.*

Another form of acceptance from his sister. Another effect of Mandy's influence or simple sisterly love and trust? Either way, he savored the moment, wondering how long it would last. How long would he want it to continue?

Chapter Five

S ilas leaned back in his chair, giving his bulging stomach a contented pat, after finishing his luncheon repast. Beside him, his aunts snickered as they laid down their spoons. "That was a fine meal."

He hadn't anticipated the rustic inn situated out in the wilds of northern Alabama would harbor decent cooking let alone the delectable offerings he'd enjoyed. Matt Simmons should call himself a wonder instead of a cook, but he was too modest to accept the compliment. Indeed, he claimed his father gave him a challenge to try to improve not only the array of items on the menu but the quality of each. He patted his stomach again as a smile spread on his lips.

"You appear very satisfied." Faith pursed her lips. "Smug in fact."

"Yes, well, it is past time for us to retire for the afternoon." Hope rose from her seat. "Bring Malachi, sister. I'm in need of a nap."

Faith grabbed up the black and white cat and with a sweep of black skirts the two witches left the dining room.

Cassie watched them leave then strode toward Silas. Her

sweet expression masked the concern swirling inside her. He detected the fine tremor evident in the way her eyes lingered on the place the aunts disappeared. As if afraid they'd reappear as abruptly as their ma.

"That's a relief." Cassie shook her head as she stopped by Silas' chair. "Now that you've stuffed your face, I have something to show you." Cassie arched an eyebrow at him. "If you're ready?"

A shadow fell across the table. Silas acknowledged the Guardian as he halted beside Cassie, resting the tips of his fingers on the table. "Where are you going?"

Tension hummed inside of Giles. Silas quickly gained his feet to peer at him. "What's the matter?"

Giles shrugged as he straightened to his full height. "I intend to keep close to our sister for her protection. There's something in the air I don't like."

"You can come, too." Cassie tilted her head toward the doorway. "Follow me."

Ma's private attic has some surprises for you.

What sorts of surprises? She didn't mention anything about surprises.

In the trunks and knick-knacks and books. Wait until you see the vast collection of artifacts and relics she's kept.

Books? Interesting.

He loved to read, to explore the world through others' experiences. To sample life through different eyes, tongues, and touches. The vast world defied him the ability to witness all it offered. He couldn't live long enough to travel to all the fascinating places.

Minutes later, Cassie pushed the bedchamber door open, hesitating just inside. He stepped past her so Giles could also enter but then halted as he sensed Cassie's anguish. She stared at the stained carpet as she sucked in a breath. Her reaction sparked awareness of where they stood. He'd ignored the significance earlier, but Cassie couldn't.

Is that where Ma fell?

She nodded slowly and let out the air she'd held inside for a beat. "I suppose I should have Flint replace the carpet. It's a reminder of what happened to her."

"What did happen? I know she was shot..."

She sucked in a breath and slowly let it out. "Like I said, I mentioned her 'treasures' and some men mistook the exaggeration as fact. They forced her in here, beat her, scared her, and when she couldn't deliver anything of value...they killed her."

Giles wrapped a muscular arm around her slender shoulders. "I'll talk to Flint about replacing the carpet. Let's do what we came to do. Where is the key?"

She slipped a hand into her skirt pocket and withdrew one with a flying owl on its head. "Right here. Let's go." She spun away from the distressing memory to hurry up the circular stairs.

Silas followed, echoes of his mother's final minutes of life, of her terror, playing in his mind like a kaleidoscope of fractured images. His sister blamed herself but shouldn't. He would try to help her overcome her misplaced guilt. Somehow.

He trailed behind her, sensing powerful magic at the top of the steps. She fiddled with the lock for a moment and then opened the door to hurry inside. Giles' calm expression afforded him some relief but still he hesitated to enter the shadowy room. Cassie crossed the flowered carpet to the small window on the far wall and opened it to let in more light and fresh air. Giles brushed past him and soon lit the lamp standing on a fancy round table underneath the window, casting soft light throughout the small room.

Cassie ignored everything else and went straight to the smallest trunk, a dark wooden thing with bronze trim and lock on the front. She flipped through the keys on the ring in her hand until she chose one.

As she slipped the key into the lock, a premonition sent shivers of panic through him. He closed his eyes against the knowing of imminent change. A turning point he'd never recover from.

"Wait!" Silas held out a hand, not understanding his own fear of what the trunk contained. "Hold a moment."

The quiet space echoed with secrets and unspoken desires. His chest throbbed from the onslaught of bitter memories and wishes unfulfilled. Whatever waited in the small trunk would force revelations into the light.

"What's wrong?" Cassie aimed concerned eyes at him. "Are you all right?"

"I don't..." The weird sensation passed and left him shaky from his inexplicable fear. He mentally shook off the effects but the knowledge stuck fast. "Sorry about that. Go ahead."

She peered at him silently for a moment. *Are you sure?*

A passing feeling. It's gone. Go ahead.

Giles frowned at him. "There's nothing scary in that trunk, just some papers and such. You've nothing to fear."

How did he know he'd been afraid? Silas shrugged at him. "I'm not afraid."

Any longer, hm? Cassie smirked at him and shook her head. "Ready?"

He simply nodded, keeping any other qualms to himself.

Too soon, she lifted the lid on the ebony trunk to expose a mass of bundled papers, letters, and broadsides neatly stacked and tied with ribbons. All emotion except delight and curiosity fled him. Silas couldn't help himself as he reached for the first stack of papers, a mix of flyers and pamphlets.

"Those look pretty old." Giles leaned closer as Silas folded his legs to sit on the floor.

"Let's see what they are." Silas pulled the ribbon loose so he could flip through them. "Here's one announcing a new clothing shop opening in downtown Montgomery twenty years ago. Another of a Shakespeare play to be performed around the same time." He set the pamphlets aside to lift a hefty stack of newsy broadsides and rest them on the floor.

"Are those newspapers?" Cassie held onto the edge of the trunk as she peeked at the print.

"From down around Montgomery, yes." He freed them from their ribbon and skimmed the articles on each page. "Look, some are starred." He pored over the typeset print and then stiffened as he made the connection between them. "These are about our family."

"How do you mean?" Giles angled his torso so he could read over his shoulder. "That's about Grandfather's death."

"It says he was murdered in retaliation for stealing property." Silas scanned the rest of the article. "It says, 'Robert Covington was suspected of being involved with dark magic but authorities could never prove such activities. However, his sudden death occurred under mysterious circumstances and fingers have been pointed at another man who is also suspected of employing witchcraft. Legend has it the two men desired and fought over the same territory but this reporter has not been able to find anyone who could confirm whether that is in fact true. Covington leaves behind three daughters.' Does that make him a legendary figure?" He grinned at Cassie, striving for a touch of levity after reading such a dark story.

"Legends of wrath from our family's secretive past." Cassie smiled back, but no humor reflected in her eyes. "Aunt Hope did say Grandfather died at the hands of another warlock."

"Seems like our family secret was suspected after all." Giles pointed to the stack of papers. "I wonder if there are more like that one."

"Hey, look at this." Cassie lifted a few sheets of paper out of the trunk. "It's music."

"What kind of music?" Silas discerned Cassie's eagerness toward the find. The girl sure loved her music.

"Some form of light verse. See, the lyrics rhyme." She studied the pages with smiling eyes. "I love to sing and use my voice to help my audience be calm and enjoy themselves. I want to use my voice for good unlike what our aunts want me to do."

"Perhaps I could write you words to a tune you could sing." He chuckled at the gleam of interest in her eyes. "I've never done that before so it would be fun to try."

"That's a wonderful idea, Silas. Thank you." She grinned at him and then peered at the sheets of paper in her hands.

"Children." Mercy shimmered into the room with a worried frown over her eyes. "Have a care with those papers."

Silas blinked at her sudden appearance and her warning. "The songs?"

"They aren't merely songs, but songspells meant to

entrap others into doing what the words demand." Mercy propped her fists on her ghostly hips as she shifted side to side in agitation. "There's a reason I kept them locked away. That's powerful magic indeed."

"I thought I might write Cassie some lyrics for her to sing for her guests." Silas flicked his brows up and then back down. "It would be a fun experiment."

"And very dangerous. You two must be careful. Remember what I said. When witches combine their talents their powers combine and increase as well."

"I wondered if that might be the case." Cassie replaced the music into the trunk and glanced at Giles. "Like when Giles played his guitar while I played the piano and sang, the effect on the audience seemed greater."

"The very reason my sisters want you to join with them, Cassie. To make their powers stronger and more dangerous. Please be careful how you combine your talents."

"I promise, Ma." Cassie held out her hands to Silas. "Let's put these back inside for now. It's getting rather late in the day."

Silas retied the ribbons and handed the stacks to Cassie. "I hadn't realized how late it's become. Flint asked me to ride out with him this afternoon for some target practice and to see the area. I need to go meet him."

Mercy floated closer to Silas, stretching a hand out toward him. "I want you to know that I've kept all these books and papers for you. Knowing your affinity with words and language, it seemed the right thing to do. You may find much to elevate your understanding of the past within the documents and books."

Silas stared at his dead mother as he absorbed the

immensity of the gift she'd preserved for him. The family history was in that trunk and on those shelves. What would he learn about his family's past? Its origins? Its hopes and dreams over the years? And his mother, who'd once actively wanted him to leave home, had kept all of it for him until he returned. She had anticipated he would eventually return to the family. Proof of her love and hope for the family's future. His heart swelled with happiness.

Even as he recalled the immense fear and panic of moments before. He stood on the verge of uncovering the truth of the family's past. How might the new knowledge impact the family relationship of the present and future?

"I deeply appreciate it, Ma. I'll treasure it always."

"I love you, son." She smiled as she shimmered and then disappeared.

"That was unexpected." Silas glanced around the space, ensuring she had vanished.

Her rapid entry and exit left him dismayed. More than he anticipated. Mixed feelings clenched his gut. The surprise of talking to his ma when he never thought to have such an opportunity. Missing her when she popped out of sight. Conflicting inside like truth and lies.

Giles folded his arms over his burly chest. "Ma is changing. She's kinder now."

"She's softening. I've noticed that, too." Cassie closed the lid and then straightened. "I wonder why."

"She actually said she loves me." Silas glanced at his brother and sister as he wrestled with the foreign concept. "I can't believe it."

Giles punched him on the shoulder, leaving a sore spot to rub away later. "Believe it."

"I'll try. But I have to leave now." Silas let his gaze fall on the ebony trunk and the many insights and secrets it contained. Intrigued by the sheaves of papers and their contents. The shelves of books called to him. But Flint awaited him so he couldn't satisfy his curiosity. "I'll come back later to see what else is in there."

Buck trotted easily down Winchester Road alongside the bay Morgan gelding Silas rode. Spending time with Cassie's youngest brother gave him a chance to assess the man. Of the four, he seemed most at ease, most curious about the world around him. The result being someone with an open mind and accepting nature. Flint appreciated him and his attitude. Over time they could become good friends. If the man stayed around. Flint pointed to a faint trail leading up the hillside into the woods. "We're nearly to the turn to the cave entrance. Just up ahead there."

"Why a cave?" Silas relaxed into the movement of his sturdy mount, evidence of the many hours he'd spent in the saddle on his travels. He'd changed into comfortable breeches and waistcoat with a gold shirt and matching softly tied cravat.

"For safety. I don't want to accidentally shoot someone passing by." Flint's preferred chocolate brown breeches clung to his legs, his cream coat and white shirt in crisp contrast. He'd chosen a cave because he couldn't imagine how terrible he'd feel in such an event. Learning how to safely fire the flintlock pistol he nearly always carried had been daunting enough. But if he shot somebody who happened to be in the wrong place at the wrong time? He shuddered with revulsion. "The foothills around here are riddled with caves, so it's handy as well."

They slowed to a walk and turned up the trail, dodging and ducking limbs edging it. After a few minutes, they emerged into a small clearing where another bay horse with a white star stood tied to a tree branch. The narrow mouth of the cave opened behind a row of low bushes, its interior walls flickering with lamp light.

Flint halted beside the other horse and dismounted, dropping to the leaf strewn ground with a muted thud of booted feet. "Barney's already here."

Silas followed suit, swinging lithely from the saddle and landing with a swirl of leaves around his black tall boots. "Nice horse."

"He's a hardy fella." Flint looped the reins around a second branch as Silas moved to do the same. "Let's go in. Ready?"

"Lead the way."

Flint strode into the cave, his eyes adjusting as he followed the sound of Barney's whistling. In a good mood, apparently. He smiled as he turned the corner around several stalagmites, their blunt columns glistening damply from the drippings of the stalactites hanging like stone icicles from the ceiling. The cool interior of the cave greeted him. Barney, dressed in light gray vest and slacks with a white shirt and slim black string tie, nestled a tin can on a rock ledge along the back wall of the larger room of the cave. His movements were precise and confident. Just like the man.

"Glad to see you can carry a tune." Flint approached his friend, hand out to greet him properly.

Barney looked over his shoulder and then approached to shake hands with Flint. "Unlike you?"

"Exactly." Flint chuckled as he gestured to where Silas

hung back a step. "Deputy Barney Parker, I'd like you to meet Cassie's brother, Silas Fairhope."

"Another one? How many of you are there?" Barney shook hands with Silas, a wry grin on his face.

"I'm the last one of the four of us." Silas returned the grin. "How do you do?"

"Very well, thank you." Barney shoved his rough hands into the front pockets of his slacks as he regarded Flint. "What do you need help with?"

"I'm just a bit rusty. I haven't had any reason to fire it and I want to make sure I can do so accurately." Flint pulled the pistol from the holster hanging from his waist and resting against his outer thigh. "I wish it were lighter but it's the only weapon I own."

"I can see why you'd want something lighter if you're going to wear it all the time." Silas studied the weapon with experienced eyes. "I could give you one of mine, if that would help."

"One?" Flint gaped at Silas. "You have how many?"

"More than enough so I could gift one to you." Silas shrugged with humor sparkling in his eyes. He reached into his coat pocket and pulled a smaller flintlock pistol out. "What? You think I'd travel without protecting myself?"

"That's unique. What kind of gun is that?" Flint had never seen such an elegant pistol.

"It's a five-shot flintlock from London. Elisha Collier, an American engineer, attained the rights and left Boston to manufacture them." Silas held the gun in his left hand, pointing out features with his right forefinger. "See, it's got a five-shot cylinder you can rotate easily and there's a priming powder magazine here."

Not only was the mechanism clever, but the pistol's

curved wood handle fitted neatly into the filigreed metal barrel. Even the trigger employed an elegant circle and curve of metal. The entire thing was beautiful as well as deadly. Flint practically drooled with envy.

"Can I see it?" Barney held out a hand. "I've heard of it but I've never seen one before."

"Of course. I ordered it last year when I saw one while in Boston on assignment." Silas turned the gun to offer the handle to the deputy.

Barney took the gun to inspect it, angling it this way and that but aimed away from the men. "How accurate is it?"

"I've never missed what I've aimed at." Silas crossed his arms over his chest. "But I don't need to use it often. It's yours, Flint, if you want it."

Flint blinked at Silas, shocked to his core. "You want to give it to me? I can't accept that. It must have been very expensive."

"I'm serious. You'll use it to help protect my sister. It's a worthwhile investment to me as a result." Silas grinned at him for a second and then sobered. "That gun will not let you down and won't wear you out, either. From what I've been told, you're going to need it at the inn."

"Not just at the inn." Barney handed the gun back to Silas. "Show us what you can do with it. Then Flint can use it for target practice."

"You know what's been happening at the inn, Deputy?" Silas lifted the pistol, pivoting to aim it at one of the targets.

"Not really. Why don't you tell me?" Barney gestured at the target. "Go ahead. Shoot."

Flint held his breath, unsure what to say to his friend as he carefully watched how Silas used the gun. Silas primed the gunpowder with the built-in device, then turned the cylinder with ease, before he pulled the trigger. The blast echoed around the stone walls of the cave as the tin can flew backward with a hole through the center of it.

"That's damn fine." Barney nodded, a smile lifting the corners of his mouth. "All right, Flint. Did you see how to fire it?"

"I think I understand, but let me know if I do something wrong." Flint held out his hand to take the weapon as Silas handed it to him.

"Then you can talk to me about the inn." Barney peered at him for a moment. "I'd bet it's about the murdered women, isn't it?"

Flint froze and stared at Barney. "Maybe. I've heard rumors that they're suspected witches. Is there any truth to that?"

Barney nodded slowly. "I've heard the same. I don't know whether it's true or not, but even if it is, that's no reason to kill those women."

"Do you believe in magic? That witches exist, I mean?" Silas asked, curiosity ringing in his tone.

Flint held his breath. He'd never dared to raise the subject with his friend. Fear of what might happen as a result of people knowing about the magic at the inn along with the other fine offerings kept him mum. He didn't want to lose a friend over some misunderstanding or worse over learning the truth of his betrothed and her family.

"I try to keep an open mind about things. My own mother was accused of being a witch once before she died unexpectedly several years ago." Barney shrugged and glanced between Silas and Flint. "I don't believe she was a witch, but who's to say whether they exist or not? Same with ghosts and other things we can't explain."

"I'm sorry about your mother. But do you believe in ghosts then?" Flint couldn't believe his ears. "Have you seen one?"

"Thanks for your condolences." Barney crossed his arms over his chest and nodded. "And yes, I've had some unexplainable things happen to and around me. Was it a ghost? Maybe."

"How did your mother die?" Silas dangled his hands at his sides but kept his gaze on the deputy. "Do you know?"

Such a loaded and personal question. An interviewer's pointed inquiry. Silas must be a fine writer, his articles likely insightful and entertaining. Indeed, he probably used his sparkling personality to pry details easily from his subjects.

"I found my mother in her house, dead in her bed. Not a mark on her." He shrugged as he dropped his hands to his sides. "I guess old age or maybe an apoplexy in her sleep. But knowing these recent killings may be because someone merely thinks the women are witches just like my mother was accused, makes me want to catch the culprit and hang him high."

"That reminds me. On my way to the inn the other day, I saw a man running from a cottage not far from here." Silas looked into the deputy's eyes, his own hard and glittering. "He might be the culprit you're looking for. I hope you catch him. Maybe for different reasons, but he needs to be stopped."

Barney heaved a sigh. "I'll check it out. Thanks for the tip."

"We can all agree then." Flint glanced at Cassie's brother and then his friend. "Whatever it takes, we need to find him."

The chill in the early evening air hinted at the coming of winter before too many more months. Silas reclined in a chair on the front porch, his hands folded on his stomach as he stared across the quiet carriageway. He'd lit an oil lamp on the table between the chairs, leaving the wick short to minimize the light it provided. The overnight guests had finally retired to their accommodations and the noisy supper rush had ended hours before. Stars dotted the darkness above, the waning moon peeking above the tree tops. He drew in a long breath and held it, listening with his ears and his senses to the world around him. Heard only the distant hoot of an owl amidst the rustlings in the pastures nearby.

It's so lovely out tonight, Cassie. Perfect for reflection.

Reflecting on his reasons for agreeing to Cassie's request. As well as the many things he'd discovered about himself and his family upon his arrival. With more to learn waiting, hiding, lurking in the attic. Should he stay until his father came home like Giles wanted him to do? Or get back on the road to the next town, the next story? He'd come all this way, it would be a shame to not see his pa. On the other hand, he had obligations to fulfill. People and places he needed to see. He cringed at the contrast between the quiet surrounding him to the symphony of sounds of a bustling city.

Enjoy your peace and quiet while you can.

He could hear the laughter in her words even without hearing her voice. She enjoyed having all her brothers home with her. She had missed all of them. Silas hadn't let himself think about what her feelings might be but now he could sense her happiness at having him and the rest of the brothers under one roof. With an eagerness to see their pa in a very few days.

Footfalls inside portended the front door opening and Matt stepping out onto the porch. Silas peered up at the cook, seeing his glimmering smile in the flickering lamplight. His lanky frame edged closer to the vacant chair and Silas motioned for him to sit down.

"That's nice." Matt sighed as he relaxed in the chair. "I've been standing far too long today."

"All your hard work is most worthwhile." Silas smiled at him and then let his gaze drift out over the gazebo with its blanket of dormant vines. A tempting destination to settle with a captivating tale on history, perhaps. "I've eaten very well. Perhaps too well."

Matt chuckled deep in his throat. "Glad to hear it. I can barely keep up with the demand. Flint's going to ask around for some more kitchen help, maybe even put a notice in the paper. If you know anybody..."

Silas brushed aside the half-hearted question. "I'm so new around here, that's unlikely. I have no idea how to hire anyone. But your experience in the kitchen is quite evident with the delectable results you've created."

"I've been cooking a long time, ever since—" Matt's gaze fixated on some point in the distance, mouth tight and hands balled into fists for a moment. "I don't talk about it much, try not to think about it, either."

Silas reached out to him with his senses, detecting his simmering anger, regret, and relief roiling inside. The intensity of the other man's emotions made Silas reflexively protect himself from the tumbling inferno. His own curiosity soared with the combination of the cook's expression and his reaction to his memories and the thoughts they evoked.

"Are you all right?" Silas asked softly.

"Fine and dandy now." Matt cleared his throat with a harsh, guttural sound. "Thanks to Giles, my life has turned out far better than when he first found me and Zander."

Silas kept quiet, giving Matt the time and space to order his thoughts, decide how much he might want to share with a complete stranger in the evening darkness.

Long practice taught him when to simply wait versus when to press for more information. He couldn't count the number of people he had spoken to over the last several years, learning their secrets, hopes, and failures as well as helping them come to terms with their own life story. Not just the snippet he was there to write but the individual person.

A long sigh preceded Matt's deep voice breaking the quiet. "We were slaves, beaten and threatened all our lives, Zander and me. That's how I got this here gap in my front teeth, the massa beat me for not working fast enough. Working the fields outside of New Orleans in the sun and the bugs ain't an easy life, believe me. We didn't know any other life since we'd been brought to the plantation as boys. Not until Giles came to deliver some goods to the massa."

"What did he do?" Knowing his older brother, anything was possible. "How did he help you?"

Giles acted as a guardian long before inheriting the title. Silas sat up straighter and rested his hands on the armrests.

"He traded the goods for us." Matt shot a frown at Silas and then focused on the gleaming crushed rock drive. "He saved our lives."

"That's my brother." Silas regarded Matt's chiseled profile for a moment. The other man stared out across the expansive front yard. "He hates slavery as much as the rest of us. We weren't raised to own another person but to respect each other. I'm glad he got you out of that dreadful situation."

"I owe him my life." Matt swiveled his head to study Silas with dark, sober eyes. "I won't do anything to disrespect him, but I do hope to do more with my life than be a cook at this here inn. I want more from my life, from my freedom to choose my future. Now that my father has found our mother, we'll be a family again, just like with you guys coming here to the inn. I have some ideas of what I want to do with my future."

"Such as?"

"Don't say I'm mad, but I want to have my own place, my own tavern perhaps. You know, a place where I can fix the foods I want to, something more casual than the fancier fare we serve here." Matt tapped the arm of the chair with a forefinger. "Not too far away, mind, so I can visit from time to time."

"That's quite an aim for your future. Do you have any idea when you'd like to accomplish your vision?"

"Oh, definitely after my father returns. He'll probably want to take over in the kitchen and now that I've run it for a spell, I don't know that I can go back to being his second." Matt stilled his finger and met Silas' amused grin. "See, I knew you'd understand. It's one thing to be with your pa but another thing to answer to him day in and day out. No sir, I want to be my own boss."

"I can well imagine how you feel, Matt." How would he react to seeing his own father return in a few days? How might his father greet him after the years apart? With joy or reserve? "I haven't seen my father in several years now. I have changed in the interim so seeing him again is bound to be an interesting event."

"My father is bringing back my newly freed mother, who I haven't seen since I was a young boy." Matt's gaze drifted away from Silas to peruse the quiet landscape before them. "She won't even know me."

Silas surveyed the surroundings, lit only by the soft moonlight reflecting off the white stone carriageway. He couldn't pretend to fathom what the other man was anticipating upon the reunion of a mother he wouldn't know any more than she'd know him. He'd grown into a strong and capable young man in the intervening years. How might she have changed?

"You'll have much to say to one another." Much like Silas had things he wanted to say to his mother, and his father upon his return. Which settled the question of whether he would stay to see his pa. "I can well imagine."

Matt nodded, his eyes on Silas. "I believe you can."

Are you still relaxed? I sense you're a bit more anxious now.

Go to bed, sis. I'm fine.

Early the next morning, Silas went for a walk to explore the property. He wandered into the barn, the sweet smell of straw and the sharp tang of horse manure greeting him. From a stall on the left he heard a man's voice murmuring and followed the sound until he spotted Flint grooming a buckskin paint horse. The rhythmic circular movements of the curry comb sent a small cloud of hair and dust into the air to the accompaniment of Flint's low voice.

"Good morning." Silas propped his folded arms on top of the half wall of the stall. He detected the innkeeper's satisfaction mingled with uncertainty. "What's his name again?"

"Buck." Flint shrugged as he worked along the horse's back toward his haunches. "Creative, hm?"

"Appropriate."

"What brings you out here so early?" Flint paused to beat the accumulated dust and hair out of the comb to drift to the straw-covered floor.

"My curiosity. I wanted to explore the property some more, see what's what."

"You've found the barn. Your horse is over there. He's quite a nice one."

"Thanks. He's carried me many a mile." Silas glanced over at Traveler, contentedly munching on a pile of hay in the corner of his stall. "I suppose it's a nice break for him to rest a few days until my father returns."

"So you're staying for a while?" Flint eased around Buck to start grooming his other side. "Cassie will be pleased."

"For a while, yes." Flint's anxiety ratcheted up at the mention of Reggie's impending return. Silas studied his taut shoulders as he continued grooming the horse. "What happens when my father returns?"

"Regarding what?"

The question rattled Flint even more, so it had to do with his father's presence at the inn. "What happens to your role here?"

A hitch in Flint's rhythm betrayed his agitation but he kept working as if nothing was bothering him. Much. Silas didn't need to be an empath to figure that much out.

"I'm not sure. I would imagine Mr. Fairhope will resume managing the place and I'll go back to help my father with the hotel in the city."

"Is that what you want?" Silas studied the man, noting the repeated slide of his Adam's apple, the tension of his hand on the curry comb. "After all you've done here?"

"That was our agreement."

"Things change, though, don't they."

Flint huffed a sigh. "Around here, all the time."

"I was talking to Matt the other night and he said you're looking for more kitchen help. Why the need?" He wanted to find out more about his future brother, wanted to keep him talking. He liked what he'd seen so far but everyone had their own secrets. Secret desires and wishes kept close to their vest like a winning poker hand. What did Flint want?

"Turns out I'm not bad at increasing business with the inclusion of new services and food choices." Flint switched to a soft bristled brush to swipe across the paint's coat to remove the layer of dirt. "Thus the need for not only additional help in the kitchen to prepare the required number of meals each day, but also several more rooms for guests to occupy at night."

"I had noticed the new wood. I'm sure Pa will be very complimentary about your efforts on his behalf." Silas sensed Flint's pleasure at the mention of his accomplishments. "Are the rooms finished?"

"Not quite, but I have a few more days and several neighbors pitching in to help." Flint rested both hands on Buck's back as he leveled his gaze at Silas. "Would you have some time to use a hammer?"

A chance to see Flint in action, see what kind of leader and businessman he actually turned out to be. "Sure thing. When do you need me?"

"Tomorrow morning is soon enough." Flint flicked a last

patch of dirt from Buck's side and then came out of the stall to stand beside Silas in the aisle. "I appreciate your stepping up to help especially since we need those rooms when your father and everyone gets here."

A veritable crowd wended their way toward the inn. Each day bringing them closer. Bringing the moment when he'd see his father again. The moment he'd have the chance to confront him regarding the truth behind his harsh actions in bygone years. Gone but not forgotten—nor forgiven. He had more to learn regarding other secrets exposed.

"Very well. That will give me some time to speak to my mother and learn more about my abilities." Silas turned to leave, then hesitated. "If I can help in any way while I'm here, please don't hesitate to tell me."

"Thanks for that. I will do so."

"And one more thing." Silas explored the contours of Flint's face, seeing the wariness despite his open expression. "I know the future may seem cloudy right now, what with my pa coming home with different expectations. But you can be certain my sister loves you and will stand by you no matter what happens. Trust in your relationship."

With that he nodded once and then strode down the aisle and outside of the barn, the weight of Flint's gaze heavy on his shoulders.

Chapter Six

*C*loudy skies cast light shadows across the carriageway later that morning. Cassie swept dust and leaves off the front porch with a new straw broom. The four dogs sprawled at the end of the porch, panting as they supervised her work. Their presence comforted her as she moved methodically down the length of the porch. They were an unlikely mix of dogs. Two Labrador retrievers, one Golden retriever, and one Cocker Spaniel—Beau and Pickles, Red, and Cocoa, respectively—to serve as watch dogs for the property. Loyal and alert but not aggressive. Her pa didn't want customers scared away, after all. He merely wanted to know when they arrived so he could ensure a proper greeting. She inhaled but didn't smell rain in the air. Still, without the sunshine, it was a melancholy sort of day. The kind where she anticipated adverse happenings.

Glancing at Teddy, she pointed at him with the top of the broom handle. "You really need to work on your math instead of reading that story."

He aimed a lopsided grin at her and turned the page. "I'm almost finished with the book, then I'll grab my slate.

Can you give me some harder problems to solve unlike last time?"

"Don't be cheeky. I'll swat your bottom with this here broom." She grinned at the boy's teasing. "Of course I will do my best to make your math problems more challenging. Now, finish your book."

She pivoted to sweep the pile of dirt toward the edge of the porch, brisk swipes of the bristles herding the bits and pieces to fall off the end of the boards into the grassy border below. After she finished the sweeping, she'd take a moment to check on her garden, determine what cleanup and winter preparations she'd need to make. Then more mending waited for her needle and thread.

Bear and Pickles leapt to their feet, barking and wagging their tales.

"Uh-oh." Teddy stood up and edged closer to her. "That's my pa coming."

She tensed at the dread threaded through his voice. Not fear so much as reluctant inevitability. Sure enough, the shambling gait of the man approaching the inn declared the wretched man as none other than Adam, the boy's no-good father. He'd had a hand in Mercy's attack even if he wasn't the one to pull the trigger. The man moved like a gaunt rag doll but his golden eyes fixated on his son. Surely he didn't intend to take the boy away. But why else would he venture to the place his crimes landed him in jail?

"What's wrong?" Giles' voice sounded beside her and made her jump. "I can tell you're either afraid or very upset."

"I didn't hear you coming." He must have sensed her concern and come out to check on her. Their connection had strengthened since Silas had arrived, supporting her mother's contention about her powers growing as they gathered together. She pointed at the man drawing nearer with each passing moment. "Adam Jacobs, Teddy's pa."

"Go inside, Teddy." Giles braced his feet apart and folded his arms over his chest. "I'll handle this."

"Won't make no difference, sir." Teddy laid the book on the table and mimicked Giles' stance. "He's come for me."

The lad stared at his approaching father. Inside of him, Cassie sensed his resistance. He wanted to stay at the safety of the inn. The routine comforted him, knowing people cared about him, looking to his needs. Unlike his father.

"Do you want to go with him?" Giles peered down at the boy.

"No, sir." Teddy chewed his lower lip for a second. "I like it here fine."

Adam kept coming but Cassie could only wish for him to turn around and leave them in peace. She hummed her calming spellsong for Teddy's benefit. The man's clothing hadn't been improved by time spent in jail. His muddy brown hair needed a good trimming and he could use a shave, too. Her pa would object to his presence looking such a disgrace. She sensed the man's annoyance when he deduced why Teddy hadn't yet descended the steps to meet him. Annoyance rimmed with anger.

"Teddy, come on down here and give your pa a proper greeting." Adam yelled across the carriageway, his reedy voice slicing through the air.

She jumped at the bark of sound despite knowing his inner state. "Don't let him take Teddy, Giles. That man abandoned his son to do his thieving."

"Please?" Teddy's eyes glistened as he looked from Cassie to Giles. "I want to stay."

"Theodore Jacobs, get down here." Adam halted at the foot of the steps, his reluctance to move within Giles' reach plain to everyone in the angling of his body.

If she recalled right, Giles had threatened the three rogues while they were being held in jail. She'd heard he nearly killed the deputy and his friend Zander in the process. The very day Giles had come fully into his superhuman strength from all accounts. Adam had good reason to be wary of Giles.

"The boy's staying put right here beside me, Mr. Jacobs." Giles rested a hand on Teddy's shoulder. "He said he doesn't want to go with you."

"He's my son and you don't get a say in what he do or don't do." Adam's anger was palpable but his fear of Giles kept him at bay. "I've done my time and now it's time for us to git on home."

She'd been right to worry about the awful man's attempt to reclaim his son, let alone interfere with the boy's education and welfare. What the man hadn't counted on was her own determination to protect the boy from harm. Harm of any kind from any direction. "He's better off with us, Mr. Jacobs. See how well he looks as evidence."

"Makes a spit of difference, miss. He's my boy and belongs with me." Adam squinted at Teddy and pointed to the ground. "Git on down here."

Hoofbeats sounded on the crushed stone drive. "Mr. Jacobs, you've no business here."

Flint led his saddled horse to the hitching rail with measured strides and tied him to it. Cassie had never been so glad to see her fiancé. He acted calm and in charge despite his inner qualms, but purpose bolstered his nerve. He wouldn't let anything untoward happen to anyone.

Including young Teddy. She sensed his resolve and relaxed a tad. Then he pulled the fancy flintlock pistol Silas had gifted him from the holster and leveled it at Adam. His way of protecting those under his care. She blinked at the sight, holding her breath and hoping he wouldn't need to pull the trigger. What if he killed the boy's father right in front of him? She grabbed Teddy's shoulders and pulled him close, prepared to shield his eyes if necessary.

"There's no need for that." Adam stepped back, eyes wary. "I mean no harm."

"From the sound of the argument I heard all the way from inside the stable, I think there is a strong need for you to be on your way." Flint flicked a telling glance as Giles sidled around so the boy and Cassie stood behind him. Then Flint aimed hard eyes at the intruder. "You forfeited any claim to the boy when you left him on his own while you went about the countryside causing mischief. You are not welcome here. If I catch you on this property again, I'll have you arrested for trespassing. Understood?"

"He's my son and I want him back." Adam scuffled his feet on the stones. "I don't want to live alone."

"That's not my problem." Flint cocked the pistol. "Now leave and don't come back."

"But—"

Flint fired the pistol at the man's feet, kicking up a spray of stones against his legs that made Adam jump sideways with a shout of pain. "I won't ask again."

Cassie clutched the boy's shoulders as she stifled the shriek trying to fly from her mouth. Flint didn't need the distraction and she wouldn't give Adam an opportunity to worsen the situation further. Flint aimed the muzzle at Adam's heart. She swallowed the bitter tang in her throat, hoping against hope Adam would walk away. Not drive Flint to kill him in order to keep his promise to protect her and those she cared for. She hummed louder, her arms tense about the boy.

"Do as he says, Jacobs." Giles took two steps forward and shooed Adam away with a sweep of one arm. "Or I'll come down there, and I know you don't want that."

"All right, all right, I'm a-goin'. You can have him and his lazy butt." Adam spun around with a glare over his shoulder as he started back down the lane toward the main road. His ambling gait was emphasized by the defeated droop of his shoulders. As he walked, he threw hateful looks over his shoulder but kept going.

After Adam was out of earshot, Flint holstered his gun and then turned to face Cassie with glittering eyes unlike any she'd ever seen. "That should be the end of that, but if he dares show his whiskers here again, you let me know. All of you."

"I doubt he'll be back." Giles moved to one side so his charges could see Flint clearly. "You did a good thing just now."

Teddy raced to wrap Flint in a bear hug. "Thank you. I'll never leave you."

Joy swept through the boy and made Cassie smile with relief and delight. "You don't have to, Teddy. You can live here with us from now on."

Teddy released Flint and raced back up the steps to hug her. "Thank you! I promise to be good and stay with you forever and ever and ever."

His anger and fear had been replaced with such a wave of relief and glee, her own heart might burst with love for the lad. She held on tight for several moments, gazing over his head at Giles and Flint watching with wide smiles on their faces. Then she planted a kiss on the top of the boy's head before setting him away from her so she could peer into his happy eyes.

"Now go get that slate and let's do some math." She spun him around and swatted his butt. "No more lollygagging about, you hear?"

He rubbed a hand on his backside and then grinned. "Anything you say, miss."

He snatched up the book and disappeared inside the inn to retrieve the slate and chalk. Cassie grabbed up the forgotten broom from the porch floor, meeting Flint's expectant gaze. She leaned the broom against a post and hurried down the steps to stand before him. She searched his expression for a moment and then kissed him lightly on the cheek.

"What was that for?" He touched the place she'd pressed her lips.

"For scaring that awful man away without injuring him." She folded her arms around her waist. "I didn't want more bloodshed, especially in front of Teddy."

He nodded slowly and then pulled her arms away to put around his neck. He lowered his head to kiss her soundly, until Giles cleared his throat in warning. A quick smirk at Giles and he kissed her again before easing her arms down. "Now that's settled, Giles and I need to ride into town to pick up the mail and some other things as well as see someone."

A chill swept through her at the thought of being left to defend herself but only briefly. She'd grown more capable after all. "Both of you?"

"We won't be long and you have your other brothers

here." Flint clasped one hand and squeezed it lightly. "Abram said he'd shift into a guard dog or a big black bear if necessary."

"That would be a sight to see." She chuckled at the image of her brother as a ferocious bear. "You're right, though. I'm sure I'll be fine with so many others around. Go on."

"If you need me, call me. I'll be back at your side in a blink of an eye, literally." Giles gave Cassie a quick hug and then trotted down the steps. "I'll get my horse and we'll go."

Flint moved to untie Buck from the hitching rail. "Hurry up, I don't want to keep him waiting any longer than necessary."

Flint didn't offer a name so she didn't inquire. If he needed her to know, he'd inform her. She trusted him to keep her apprised of what she needed to know. Still, taking Giles meant something serious weighed on Flint's mind.

"Be right back." Giles spun on his heel and strode briskly across the carriageway to the stable.

Cassie watched him until he entered the shadowy building, all while considering how to satisfy her curiosity. "Why do you need Giles to go with you, Flint? You usually ride in alone."

"We need to talk about something where others can't hear." He grimaced as he shrugged one shoulder. "Men talk. We won't be long, though."

Giles emerged from the stable leading one of the inn's horses as he'd lent his to Zander for the journey to Georgia. He halted outside the doorway and mounted with fluid grace for such a burly man. He urged the horse into a walk and approached Flint.

"We've got to go, but don't worry." Flint swung up into

the leather saddle and picked up the reins. "It's not anything to make you fret." He hesitated and then eased a small smile onto his lips. "You know I love you."

"Yes, and I love you." She sensed his reluctance to share the topic of conversation but also his intent to protect her from any bad news he might be worried about. He wanted to protect her even from that. "See you later."

He waved and reined his horse around to join Giles as they trotted down the lane. She watched them go until they turned onto Winchester Road heading toward Huntsville. Then she released the sigh and started sweeping again. Stewing over the mysterious errand served no good purpose. Better to keep busy until they returned.

The sun hung high above, out of sight still behind gray clouds, as Flint rode his horse beside Giles on the road into town. For many minutes the only sound between them had been the creak of leather and the rhythmic hoof beats of the two horses on the hard-packed, dusty road. Flint chided himself for putting off the conversation he needed to have with the oldest Fairhope brother. Quailing at the idea of baring his insecurity. Took a breath and let it out slowly.

"I've been meaning to speak to you about something." There, he'd started the damn discourse. He glanced at Giles, espied the querying raised brow. "It's about your sister, actually."

"What about her?" The deep voice didn't reveal the big man's thoughts on the topic.

"I intend to marry her."

"Yes."

"Do you approve? Honestly?" He held his breath, afraid

of the answer. Afraid of being told he didn't measure up, didn't qualify to be included in their family. He had such limitations compared to the special abilities each of them possessed. Nothing special about him. Cassie had tried to reassure him but she was biased since she professed to love him. But Giles wasn't under any such illusion. On top of everything else, he may soon be out of a job. Then what? So many questions and no easy answers. He swallowed hard, trying to dislodge the sudden knot in his throat. The man would be his brother by marriage. His opinion mattered more than Flint realized until that moment.

"Flint Hamilton, you will be a fine husband for my sister. Of course I approve." Giles shook his head at him. "Stop doubting yourself."

"I don't have anything special to offer her or the family." He let out a breath along with his worst fear.

Giles reined to a halt, forcing Flint to stop and turn around. "Now listen to me. You have plenty to offer this family, especially my sister. You offer your love and support, your honesty and industry. Just because you don't have any magical talents doesn't lessen the gifts you do have."

Flint crossed his wrists on the saddle horn, Buck shifting beneath him. "Is that enough?"

"You cannot give more than you possess, and I know you will bring all of you to the marriage." Giles muttered something and urged his mount into a walk. "Enough doubting. Put it behind you and let's get to town. We promised to be back quickly."

"If you say so." Relief was sweet in his chest. If Giles believed Flint would be a satisfactory husband then he'd relax and focus on doing so. Or at least try. Flint fell in beside Giles as they picked up a trot.

A while later they arrived at the post office on a busy corner off the square in downtown Huntsville. Flint swung out of the saddle and tied the reins to the hitching rail in front of the two-story house where the mail was collected and dispatched to other towns. He scanned the list of names of recipients fixed to the outside wall of the building, spotting his and Cassie's names. He turned to where Giles remained mounted on the sturdy black gelding.

"Looks like your sister has a letter, too. Be right back." Flint acknowledged Giles' grunt of understanding with a flick of his hand. Then strode quickly into the building and turned left into the small front room of the house serving as the town's post office.

A swarthy-skinned man with a slash of a mustache greeted him with a smile. "Good morning, sir. How may I help you?"

"I'm Flint Hamilton, and you are?" He stuck out his hand to shake with the stranger.

"John P. Neale, newly appointed Postmaster General." John shook his hand with a firm grip.

"Congratulations. I saw on the list outside that you have mail for me and for my fiancé, Cassandra Fairhope."

"Congratulations to you, too, on your engagement." John turned to the array of cubbyholes mounted on the wall, trailing a hand across the small openings until he found the letters he sought. Then he crossed to a table by the opposite wall and lifted a stack of magazines and papers. "Here you go."

Flint received the stack of letters, the top one addressed to him from the high-brow hotel that had offered him a position coveted by many hostelers. Such a temptation and flattering. He had to wait for Reggie's return before he'd have an answer.

"By the way, this place is far too small to serve any longer," John said, straightening a stack of magazines, "so soon I shall be moving the post office over to a storefront along McKinley's Row. I'll announce the exact location and date of the move in the paper, so keep an eye out."

"I'll do that." Flint glanced around the crowded room, the tables piled with stacks of packages, letters, magazines, and more. The post marking stand waited on a small table shoved into the corner. A fellow could barely turn around in the cramped space. "I can appreciate the need to find larger quarters since the town population is growing as well."

"Indeed it is. Seems every day there is a new building being raised, more men arriving to try their hand at agriculture of one kind or another." John shrugged lightly. "But then again why wouldn't they want to enjoy the fine climate and abundance this state offers?"

"Very true. Well, thanks for the mail and the information. I must be off." Flint touched his fingers to his hat and then hurried out of the post office to rejoin Giles. "All right, are you ready to find Barney?"

"Actually he asked that we wait here a moment while he finds the sheriff." Giles relaxed in the saddle as comfortable as if he was sitting at home by a roaring fire.

"So he found us." Flint put the papers and magazines in his saddlebag and then flipped through the letters. "Here's one from your father to Cassie. I wonder what he has to say."

"I'm sure she'll tell us." Giles glanced down the wide street.

Flint followed his gaze, late morning shadows pooled at the base of the smattering of trees planted along the sides. Women in daytime attire and protective cloaks strolled beside men in suits and business attire, all going about their business with a sense of urgency and purpose. The town grew steadily with each passing month, more people, more businesses, more families.

Giles lifted his chin. "Here they come."

Flint spotted the two lawmen striding toward him. "It looks serious."

"More trouble, most likely."

Deputy Parker stopped beside him as Flint shoved the letters into the saddle bag and buckled it closed. Flint met his serious gaze. "What's wrong?"

"After Silas mentioned what he witnessed, you know, a large man in black running away from a cottage, we rode out to see what we could find. We found the woman dead in her living room, the door wide open." Stephen Neal slowly shook his head, his brimmed hat shading the murky light from his eyes. "This wasn't a mile from the inn so it makes us wonder. What do you know about these murders?"

Flint blinked once, unsettled by the sharp question, and then looked up at Giles. The time had come. They had to say something. "Obviously not who we thought it was. I think we should tell them what we suspect."

Giles nodded, his gaze flicking between the three men peering up at him. "Go ahead."

"We think the group of men who have started meeting at the inn may be behind the killings." Would the two serious officers of the law staring at him, waiting for him to continue, believe what he had to say? Barney would consider it but Flint didn't know Stephen well enough to anticipate his reaction. "I've heard them talk about troublesome women and having to take care of them. We think they believe the women are practicing magic."

Stephen's eyebrows shot up. "Witches? You think these men, whoever they are, are killing women they think are witches?"

"Yes. That's exactly what we suspect." Flint splayed his hands briefly before untying his horse's reins from the hitching rail. "We don't have any evidence other than our observations of the growing number of men and how frequently they've taken to gathering in the dining room. Like they're watching us."

"It's something we can look into." Barney gave Flint a long searching look. "I wish you'd told me your suspicions earlier. You know you can trust me to back you up."

"I wanted to, my friend. Sincerely." The disappointment in Barney's expression punched Flint's gut. "I'm sorry I didn't. We wanted to be certain before we pointed any fingers. We'd thought it might be a certain man but the description you gave doesn't match."

"It sounds like maybe they're taking turns." Giles offered his opinion in a gravely voice. "That way no single man would be identified and thus caught."

Stephen sighed and tapped a hand against his thigh. "The fleeing man had a mask on as well, making identifying him or them, if more than one, even more difficult."

"We need to get back to the inn, and fast. Especially now that we know of yet another killing right down the road." Giles sat up straight and lifted his reins, preparing to ride.

"Anything else you need from us?" Flint placed a foot in

the stirrup and swung into the saddle. "We do have to go to ensure our own women are safe."

"Are they suspected witches?" Barney studied Flint's tense expression. "You know my mother was suspected even though she wasn't one. So?"

"Yes, in fact." Flint gathered his leather reins in cold fingers, aware his equivocal response could be interpreted in various ways but still reluctant to say too much. "That's why we must go."

A cacophony of banging echoed within the new addition walls. Silas hefted the hammer and tapped the nail into the molding around a door frame. After several hits he realized the nail had balked at being forced into the hard wood. He hit it harder and the slender board split around the nail into tendrils of pine.

"Gadzooks!" Silas dropped the hammer to the floor at his feet in a back bedroom. "I'm no good at this."

Abram stood from where he'd been installing the last of the floor boards in the upstairs hallway then crossed to the doorway where his brother worked. "What?"

Silas pointed at the ruined wood. "I'm definitely not a carpenter."

"Don't let Flint see that, he's stressed enough about finishing on time." Abram stepped closer and used the claw end of his hammer to pry the board off and drop it to the floor with a clatter. "If at first you don't succeed..."

"You needn't remind me." Silas clomped over to the stack of narrow lengths of pine and selected a new piece. "I am improving, slowly."

"How long have you been working with wood like this?"

Abram resumed working on the final floor board, tossing an amused grin at Silas.

"Mere days, to be honest." Examining the molding, Silas carried it to the sawhorses set up in the middle of the passage. He measured and marked the board, then applied a handsaw to cut it to suit. Walking back to the doorway under the watchful and humor-filled eyes of Abram, he placed it and then nailed the top in place.

"You'll get the hang of it before we're finished here." Abram pounded the last nail head level with the board, surveyed his handiwork, and then rose to his feet. "You're renowned for your words not your woodworking."

"Probably a good thing."

The deep chuckle behind Silas made him look over his shoulder to spot Giles striding down the long hall stretching from the addition to the stairs. Curiosity gleamed in the twinkling eyes as the burly man filling the passage drew nearer.

"What's a good thing?" Silas braced for a sarcastic rejoinder from his oldest brother.

Giles glanced at the shattered board on the floor nearby and then grinned at Silas. "Words seem easier for you to manage."

"Hmph." Silas slipped a nail from a pocket on the work belt around his waist. Without further comment, he carefully secured the molding in place. Then turned with a triumphant smirk. "There."

Giles guffawed. "I'm proven wrong. Still, it's good to emphasize one's strengths instead of weaknesses."

"And to expand one's skills." Whether or not he'd ever need to work with wood again, now Silas had more confidence in undertaking such a project. He also gained a better understanding of the process of working with wood to build things. Which brought up another question he'd been pondering the answer to. "So if you think I should focus on my words, what do you think I should write next?"

"What do you want to write about?" Giles turned to inspect the progress the neighboring men had made with putting up the walls of the hall.

Silas pulled a paper measuring tape from his work belt to determine the length of molding needed for the top piece. As he stretched it across the top of the doorway, he considered his brother's question. "Something about my journey here? Or how I feel about being here with family again?"

"Hm..." Giles checked the firmness of the connection of the wall board and then paused in his task. "What about something about the family, surely someone should write a Fairhope family history."

"What's so special about our family that it needs its history captured in words?" Abram asked as he let his gaze drift over the hall.

Silas let Abram assess what else needed to be finished in the passageway while he thought about the insightful question. What was special about the Fairhope family? Let him count the ways. In fact, a trunk full of possible new ways teased his curiosity. Soon he'd go back to the attic and spend some time perusing the plethora of secrets ensconced there.

Giles chuckled as he resumed moving around the space to ensure everything had been done to Flint's exacting orders. "With all the secrets, all the special abilities, as well as the hazards we're facing and how we'll use our powers to defeat them, there must be a story in there somewhere."

"You beat me to it." Silas nodded, as ideas flooded his brain. "There's truth to what you say. A family history may be the exact thing to write before I hit the road again."

An honest review of who the people were who started the family. The kinds of options and decisions they made. The effects of those choices and how they led to other opportunities and challenges.

Giles froze for a moment and then moved to the next section of wall, running a hand over the planed wood. "Plenty of fodder, I'm sure."

Silas sensed his big brother's hesitation as well as detect it in his rigid stance and the fact he kept his gaze averted because of his inspection. Giles enjoyed the role of Guardian, or being the head of security for the family, for the inn. He felt content and happy and as Silas probed a tad farther he read Giles' intent to stay in the area for the foreseeable future.

The very concept of settling down was as foreign to Silas as the idea of moving to Egypt. While he relished his travels, riding from here to there, meeting interesting and intriguing people, experiencing new sights and foods, he had no desire to board a ship to other distant lands. He'd rather have a horse beneath him, his belongings in a saddle bag behind him and an open road before him. He'd only been staying at the inn for days and yet had this antsy feeling prodding him to move on to the next assignment.

Before he saddled up, though, he'd compile a history of how the family formed, decided to live in southern Alabama, and then for his parents to move to northern Alabama. What had prompted such major shifts in residence? How did the family left behind react to their departure? What was life like for his parents and sister? His brothers and their reasons for journeying to the Fury Falls Inn and Cassie. Sure, he'd heard some surface-level answers to those questions, but in his experience the first answers hid the raw truth like lacquered paneling hid the rougher wood beneath. Maybe learning more about their history would help everyone move forward to a new and better future. They'd be able to determine their unique role within the family structure if he could discover more insights about how the family had functioned before the schism forced everyone to separate. Then he'd have brought the family together before he went on with the rest of his life. Yes, a fine goal. Surely no one could object.

Chapter Seven

After several hours of hammering, Silas ventured outside to stroll about the yard and enjoy the late morning sunshine. He'd completed the task Flint had set for him and promised to return in the afternoon to continue. But for the moment, he needed air and light. He tipped his hat to several arriving guests and then pointed his feet toward the front yard and the inviting gazebo.

Upon his arrival days before, the gazebo had attracted his attention. He hadn't had much time to himself in the ensuing days to investigate it, so decided to spend a few quiet moments alone within its shady confines. He sauntered closer, each stride releasing the tension in his frame. He breathed deeply, letting each inhale and exhale still the building agitation. He couldn't help but feel like he needed to mount up and ride away. That was his normal routine. Stay a few days and move on. He'd been at the inn for three full days and now intended to stay until his father returned. However long that might be. He might lose his sanity in the interim.

As he neared the gazebo he noted a figure seated on

one of the three white metal benches arrayed around the interior. Head bowed, he could only discern that the person was female with long red hair about her slender shoulders. Who might she be?

He hesitated at the foot of the few steps up to the floor. "Excuse me, miss, do you mind if I join you?"

She lifted her head and her green eyes dazzled him. "Not at all. There is plenty of room."

"Thank you." He tipped his hat as he climbed the steps. "I will not interrupt your reading further."

He sat on the bench at the opposite side of the gazebo, prepared to quietly reflect on his own thoughts. One thing he'd grown very accustomed to was entertaining himself among a group of strangers. Relying on others to provide scintillating conversation or any other form of engagement had proven elusive. Better to have a list of topics ready to explore on his own, in his own way.

The lady resumed perusing the open book on her lap, her slender fingers turning the pages. Her attire bespoke her country town sensibilities, a lynsey-woolsey dress with a flowered scarf about her neck and tucked into her bodice. While pretty, she couldn't compete with other women of his acquaintance. Not that her appearance mattered to him since he'd be leaving in a week or so anyway. He had no interest in striking up a romantic relationship to tie him down.

"If you're going to continue to stare at me, then please explain yourself." Those green eyes pierced into his soul with an unrepentant gaze. She gripped the book with tense fingers. "I won't endure your examination any longer."

"My apologies. I didn't mean to stare." Silas inclined his head and then removed his hat. "My name is Silas

Fairhope. I'm the owner's son. And you are?"

"Wilma Hamilton. We've already met." She closed the book and smiled at him. "Do you recall? It was your first day here. There were so many of us, so it's understandable."

He searched his memory for a moment and then grinned at her. "I do. In the dining room the other day. You're going to marry Daniel, correct?"

"Yes, after my sister marries next month. I do not wish to upstage her with a wedding before she's safely wed." She shifted her hands on the binding of the book. "Her special day should be exactly that."

"How thoughtful of you." He regarded her pleasant features for a beat. How much did the girl know about the family? He sensed her generous nature, acceptance, and contentment. Was that because she had been kept in the dark about Daniel's timeskipping and bouncing? Or despite knowing about it? "And are you well aware of Daniel's...special gifts?"

She bestowed a small smile in answer to his hesitant question. "I am. Yours, as well."

He arched a brow and guffawed in return. "I sense that. Do you also have special abilities?"

"Not like you, but I am a fair shot with a bow and arrow. I adore archery and have even won ribbons for my skill." Her smile widened as Silas nodded at her. "I may not be able to help protect the family with magic, but I will defend everyone with my weapon of choice."

He stiffened at the steely conviction in her tone coupled with the determination and fierce love for her man in her soul. She might not possess magic, like she admitted, but her love and talents could prove fearsome indeed.

Love. He didn't expect to ever feel that emotion for a woman. For his brothers and sister, yes. His parents as well. But familial love seemed to be very different than romantic love. Settling down, with or without a woman, simply wasn't in the cards for him. He'd discovered how antsy he became when forced to stay in one place for very long. He honestly didn't envy people who never traveled, who didn't take the opportunity to explore other places and see other sights. Traveling satisfied his wanderlust and he couldn't imagine denying himself the pleasure of that satisfaction. The source of his own contentment. But how could he balance his need to mount his horse and the need to wait for his father to return?

A refreshing breeze puffed through the curtains at the front windows in the family parlor later that afternoon. Temperatures remained mild and comfortable for the middle of October. With Allhallows only a couple of weeks away, Cassie eagerly anticipated her father's arrival and the conversation they would have. She had so many questions for him, not least of which what to do to make her aunts leave her alone. Even when they weren't in sight, she felt their presence looming over her.

She'd taken over the back corner of the room with a folding table piled with articles of clothing and a straight-backed chair where she worked on the mending for the growing number of customers. She appreciated the pin money she earned but the amount of stitching took up a good deal of her free time. At least with fall coming and winter hard on its heels she had less to do in her garden. What would she do come spring?

"Can you check my work, please?" Teddy sat on a padded chair by the fireplace, squinting at the black slate in his hands.

"One moment." She finished the stitch and set aside the collar she was repairing. Then rose from her hard seat and walked across the painted floor boards to take the slate from the lad to scrutinize his mathematical calculations. "The first two are correct but the third one is not. Three times five isn't twelve, that would be three times four. So if you have three fives how many do you have in total?"

"I dunno." He hung his head, looking away from her. "I guess I'm not very smart."

"Teddy, look at me." She struggled to keep her expression neutral as the embarrassed boy slowly rotated his head. "You are smart and you can do this. Now, look at your hand. How many fingers do you have?"

"One, two, three, four, five." He counted them off and then shrugged. "So?"

"Continue counting on your other hand. How many total do you have?"

"Six, seven, eight, nine, ten."

"That's two sets of five or two times five equals ten. Now add one more set." She gently pushed confidence toward him as he struggled to follow her logic. "What do you get when you add a third set of five?"

"Fifteen?" He grinned at her. "I get it now. Multiplication is like adding, only faster."

"Yes. Keep working on the rest of the problems while I finish my mending for the day."

The front door opened which drew her attention to where Flint and Giles entered the parlor. Flint carried a stack of papers and letters, piquing her curiosity. Might he have a letter from her pa? News of his homecoming soon? He crossed the room to give her a quick kiss while Giles closed the door behind him.

"Welcome home. You were gone a while." She resumed her seat and picked up the collar to finish closing the torn seam. "I see you had mail."

"And a letter from your father. I have some other news after I take this to my desk. I'll be right back." He handed her an envelope and then turned to walk into his office.

Giles chose a cushioned chair across from Teddy, relaxing back as he watched the boy work. She watched him out of the corner of her eyes for a moment and then focused on the missive in her hands. Opening it, she devoured its contents, smiling as she finished reading what he'd written.

"Good news?" Giles crossed his ankles in front of him.

"News to share with the rest of the family. Can you please round up everyone and bring them here? I need to finish this collar and then I'll tell everyone what Pa has to say."

Giles pulled his feet under him and stood. "Everyone?"

"Just the family for this one if you don't mind. No need to interrupt everyone." They could then share with the rest. Besides, trying to include everyone on the spur of the moment would cause complications for the operation of the inn. "Thank you."

"I'll be back in a few minutes." Giles strode to the side door leading onto the covered passage.

"Finish up, Teddy. I've called a family meeting and everyone will be coming."

"Yes, miss." Teddy scratched several strokes with the white chalk on the black slate. Then set both on the table beside him. "All done."

Within fifteen minutes her brothers and aunts had trickled in, arraying themselves in the various seats around the room. Flint pulled a chair over beside the cushioned seat Cassie had chosen to occupy. A fire snapped in the fireplace, its orange and red flames licking the small pile of logs and scenting the air. She scanned the expectant faces regarding her, aware of their curiosity and impatience.

"Thank you for answering my request for a family meeting." She glanced around the room to make sure everyone had arrived before she started to read the letter. "Where's Ma? She'll want to hear this as well."

Giles sat up straight in his chair and took a breath. "Ma, we need you!"

Mercy shimmered into sight with a frown. "You don't need to bellow, Giles. I can hear you."

"At least you didn't startle anyone this time." He grinned at her and sank back in his seat. "Now we're ready."

Cassie shook her head slowly at her oldest brother. "You're incorrigible."

"What did you want us for?" Silas leaned forward, resting his elbows on his knees. *You could have just told me.*

That would defeat my purpose. She fluttered the single page of stationery. "To read this to you all at once so I won't have to repeat myself. Shall I?"

"Please." Daniel made a rolling motion with one hand.

She held the page between her hands and began to read.

Saturday, Oct. 6, 1821
My dear Cassie,

I'm pleased to tell you that my caravan is on the road at last, coming home with wagonloads of furniture pulled by pairs of oxen. I wanted to send you a brief note while we're stopped somewhere in Georgia at a tavern to repair a wheel. At the pace we're traveling, I anticipate arriving by the 29th day of October, possibly sooner if Fate will permit us to. As I mentioned in my last, I'm bringing not only Sheridan's long lost wife, Pansy, but also my brother Beck and my youngest sister Scarlet. Both have chosen to visit for an extended time, possibly to move to Alabama, based on my description of the area and opportunities. I've written to Flint with this news as well so he can allocate comfortable accommodations for them.

Give my regards to my sons. See you in a couple of weeks.

Love,

Your father

She folded the page and slipped it back into the envelope. "So, what do you think?"

"It's wonderful to hear that Beck and Scarlet will visit for a time." Mercy floated over the floor boards as she slowly spun to look at each of her sons. "You'll like them both."

Hope huffed. "They could only be coming because Reginald told them he needed their help."

"Help?" Silas stood up and peered at Hope. "Why would he do that?"

"Because he's afraid of us." Hope folded her arms as she shifted her gaze to each astonished face in the room.

"He's not afraid of you." Mercy glared at her sister, anger flaring in her glittering eyes. "Neither of us are."

"Then why did you hide your children's abilities from

us? Hm?" Faith cackled and flicked a hand up in the air. Her eyes glittered as she assessed the others gaping at her. "I think he's bringing reinforcements specifically because he knows we're more powerful than he is."

Giles also stood up and propped his fists on his hips. "But he has all of us to back him up."

Cassie glanced at the glare-off happening right before her eyes and shuddered. The future she envisioned in that moment was one filled with hate, anger, and violence. A screech preceded Allegro flying through the open window and making a circuit of the room, his sleek blue-gray wings flapping as he came to alight on her shoulder. She stroked his head as he nudged her neck to comfort her.

"Do not underestimate my husband's power, sister." Mercy continued to glower at Hope and Faith. "If you're uncomfortable with his brother and sister coming here, you're free to leave. In fact, I invite you to vacate the premises immediately so we can live in peace."

"Not without Cassandra." Hope stood and paced toward Mercy's ghost.

Anticipating another fight between the sisters, Cassie started humming her calming songspell to try to ease the tensions in the room. Hope took two more steps and then halted, pivoting to look incredulously at Cassie. Lifting a hand, she stared at her. Cassie stopped humming at the implication of that raised finger ready to bind her powers again.

"Don't you dare!" Mercy solidified in a flash of anger and flew at Hope, pushing her backward several steps before Hope landed on Daniel's lap.

Mercy shimmered and then became solid as she started toward her sister again. Giles stepped to intercede before they came to blows but Hope scrambled off Daniel's lap and made a dash at Mercy.

"Ladies, please." Abram jumped to his feet but hesitated to put himself between the two angry women. "Take a breath. We're all members of the same family."

"Not by choice." Mercy's translucent figure wavered with anger. "You've always tried to control me and now you can't so you're after my daughter. I won't let you succeed."

"It's not your decision. It's your daughter's." Faith stood beside Hope, a detaining hand on her arm. She flashed a look at Hope and then at Mercy's aggressive figure. "But I agree you shouldn't be attacking either of us. It's not fitting."

"I'll show you what's not fitting!" Mercy shifted side to side and then solidified again.

"Stop it. All of you." Cassie inserted herself between her mother's ghost and her aunts. "Behave yourselves or so help me God I'll find a way to make the two of you regret ever coming here. Now go to your room, Aunt Hope and Aunt Faith, and Ma, go away to wherever you go. I don't want to see any of you for the rest of the day." Allegro flapped his wings to keep his balance on her shoulder as she turned her frown to each of the women in turn.

Hope opened her mouth but noted the hard frown on Cassie's lowered brow and thought better of it. Which didn't stop the dangerous look aimed Cassie's way. Hope took Faith's hand, practically dragging the younger sister with her. Startled and insulted, Hope and Faith stomped past her brothers and up the stairs to their bedroom without another word. Cassie looked at her ma until the ghost shimmered out of sight.

"That was entertaining." Giles slowly sank back onto the chair. "I didn't know you had that much spunk, sis."

Her hands trembled as she resumed her seat. "Me either. They make me so mad, though."

"It's only a short time until Pa arrives and he'll be able to find a way out of this mess we're in." Silas paced the floor, his hands clasped behind his back. "I hope."

"I think we're all hoping Pa will know what to do." Abram went to the fireplace to add another log on the fire, sparks flying up the chimney.

"There's only one thing I don't know at this point." Cassie slowly shook her head as she gazed at each man arrayed around her. "What on earth do we do if he can't?"

Chapter Eight

The clouds relinquished their dominance of the heavens overnight, allowing the sun to brighten the trail leading up to the falls. Silas ambled up the gentle hill, relishing time alone before the mid-afternoon repast in the dining room. Matt had whispered to him that he'd acquired some pomegranates and dried apricots for a new baked pheasant concoction. The idea made Silas' mouth water. He dragged his fingertips across his lips to wipe the moisture away.

Rustling in the underbrush stopped his forward momentum to seek its source. A flock of turkeys scratched and pecked their way across a small clearing, their wings blending with the browns and dark golds of the fallen leaves and dry grasses. Dark orbs peered about, necks craning to assess the level of danger or find a choice tidbit as they eased through the field. He held his breath, stilling his movements to observe their progress without scaring them into flight. His heart thudded in his neck, senses tuned to his surroundings so much he almost felt he could detect the birds' wariness. Or was he merely observing it through their actions?

"Oh, that's amusing!"

The laugh that followed the shout startled the turkeys into flight, running and flapping until they disappeared into the forest.

Annoyed, Silas spun about while pinpointing the cause of the disturbance. He jogged up the trail until he came to another clearing on the opposite side of the dirt path. In the center of the grassy space, he spotted Daniel grinning at a porcupine. The short-legged beast lumbered about in a lopsided circle, its pointed snout wagging to and fro while its white-tipped spines fanned out in a lethal display. Wait. Not lumbering, but...dancing? He reached out with his senses, worried his brother flirted with disaster, and then relaxed. Abram.

"What are you guys up to?" Silas left the trail, picking his way over the rough ground, to reach Daniel.

"Just practicing." Daniel gestured to the spiney animal. "I've never seen one of those do a jig before. It's funny, isn't it?"

"Surely you could come up with something more useful." Silas slowly folded his arms. "A horse perhaps?"

"He's done that. Made a lovely Morgan just like yours. And a black bear. That was rather scary, if I hadn't known it was my brother, I mean." Daniel propped his fists on his hips. "All right, Abram. That's enough, don't you think?"

The porcupine shivered, rocking its spines, and then Abram stood in its place. He smoothed his ruffled hair down with one hand, a sly grin on his lips. "I suppose that will do for the day."

"Do you often come out here to practice?" Silas glanced about the clearing. "Someone could be lurking in the underbrush, watching everything you're doing."

"Why would they?" Abram shrugged. "Surely, going up to the springs is far more interesting than standing around here."

"Let me show you there's nothing to worry about." Daniel waggled his brows at him as he grabbed hold of his arm.

"What—"

A rushing filled Silas' ears, obscuring any other sound for several rapid beats of his heart. When the roar stopped, they stood by a small building next to the hot springs. Surrounded by large flat rocks, the pool of soothing mineral water launched wisps of steam into the air. A cluster of pines provided a privacy screen between the water and the trail. The foothills rose up behind the spring, stretching as far as he could see. An inviting retreat worthy of a visit. No wonder business boomed.

"See? Nobody here." Daniel grinned at him.

"You could have warned me." Silas ran a shaky hand through his hair. "That was a wild ride."

Feeling disoriented and off-kilter never made him happy. He strove for balance and composure. Otherwise his ability to adequately perceive and interpret the situation diminished.

"Do you want to walk back or let me bounce us back?"

"May as well bounce, I guess." He drew in a breath, steeling himself for the return trip. "What do I do?"

"Just hold on to my arm." Daniel crooked his arm toward Silas. "I'll do the rest."

Seconds later they were standing in front of Abram once more. Silas shook his head to clear away the ringing in his ears. "You have a surprising talent."

"It took me a while to really understand how to control

it, but now it's pretty smooth. Thanks partly to Abram's help." Daniel punched Abram on the shoulder. "He insisted we travel together to make sure I could help Cassie should she ever need to be transported to safety in a hurry."

"Though we hope we'll never need for him to evacuate her, it's good to be prepared." Abram reached down to tear off a blade of grass, its long tan stalk flicking about in his fingers. "Together we should be able to assist as needed."

Unlike Silas. He could only wrangle words to form spells for Cassie's benefit. How would that help her if she were caught in a trap or faced the witch hunter? A reason must exist for him to have the ability to craft potent spells. To have a seemingly magical way with words. He'd mastered language and succeeded with the written words to educate and entertain. But to protect?

"I suppose your life as a writer is far different than anything I can imagine." Abram twiddled the blade with jerky movements. "What was it like?"

His writer life continued, merely on hold not abandoned into the past tense.

"The simplest way to describe my life is that it's filled with freedom. I've traveled most of the states, met hundreds of people, and eaten in even more taverns and inns." Each one had its good aspects and questionable ones, but he always came away with a new experience, a new story to tell. "There's nobody waiting at home to chide me for being late or not returning when I said I would. I can eat and drink what I desire and not be obliged to cater to someone else's preferences."

"On the flip side of that, my dear misguided brother, having nobody at home to miss you or care for you can be a detriment." Daniel tapped a finger on his crossed arms. "I long for the day when Wilma will be that someone for me."

"I do not envy you, Daniel, only because I do not wish to settle down yet. If ever."

Abram nodded sagely as he twiddled the stem. "I felt that way, as well. Until I came here and met Mandy. Then everything changed. I plan to stay in the region, become a resident in time."

"What will you do if not settle down?" Daniel stilled his restless hands. "Do you have a plan?"

"I'm working on one. For now, I'm biding time until Pa gets here. Then I'll figure out where I'll go next."

"You could stay." Abram snapped the dry stem in half. "Or not."

"You do intend to be here until we resolve the crisis facing the family, don't you?" Daniel shifted his weight, folding his arms across his chest. "We need everyone to work together."

On one hand, Silas wished he felt as comfortable with the idea as his brothers. Having the opportunity to grow close to his brothers again, his sister, and maybe even his father, sounded fine. On the other, his gut roiled at the very idea of becoming a resident as Abram so easily stated. Where would ideas come from for his writing, his articles and essays? Living in the wilds of Alabama couldn't possibly provide the inspiration he craved and contacts he relied upon. The flock of turkeys provided a moment of quiet reflection, sure, but not enough to write an interesting article or even a short essay. Despite his brothers' attempt to help him feel welcome and accepted, he knew in his heart of hearts that he didn't belong with them. Not really.

"I will stay for a time, do not worry." Silas turned and started walking back to the trail to head to the inn for his dinner. He'd had enough of the conversation and the simmering disappointment flowing from his brothers. "Right now, it's time to eat."

The banging of hammers competed with the harsh hiss of saws through lumber. Flint dropped several planks on the floor near where the men worked. He paused to wipe his brow with a rag, then tucked it into his back pocket. The new addition needed the interior walls built to divide the space into four rooms with a center hallway on the upper floor. The lower floor had the hall at the front of the building to align with the rest of the structure. The four new rooms flanked a short passage running perpendicular to the main hallway. Then the flooring needed to be placed and rough wood walls covered with paneling. After that the finishing work of molding and trim. But he hadn't been able to find anyone qualified to do the more meticulous carpentry as everyone was already busy on other jobs in the prosperous, expanding town.

He paced through the downstairs, supervising the work of the Fairhope brothers and a couple of neighboring men who needed to earn some money. The plans for the open house coupled with an Allhallows Eve gathering perked right along. Still, Flint wanted the interior of the new addition finished and ready to receive guests. Giles was the only one not present with a hammer or saw to hand, preferring to remain close to Cassie after the sheriff's warning. Only a few more days before Reggie would arrive and Flint wanted Cassie safe and well when he walked through the front door. If he could also showcase the new addition to his boss, all the better.

"Do you need anything, Daniel?" Flint stopped beside the young man placing a length of lumber upright where one of the walls forming the hallway would stand.

With several strikes of the hammer on the cut nail heads, Daniel secured the board. He cradled the hammer head in the palm of his other hand. "I think I'm covered for now."

Teddy picked his way through the construction site lugging a bucket of water and a metal cup. Flint nodded to him in greeting and appreciation for thinking of the hard-working men. The lad disappeared around a stack of lumber. The boy's future rested in his hands now that he'd banned his father from contacting him. Cassie's concerns for the lad's education echoed in his mind.

As Flint turned back to Daniel, an idea hit him upside the head. Something which should have been an obvious avenue of inquiry. "I have a question for you."

"What?" Daniel tapped a nail into place.

"Who should I ask about school options for Teddy?" Flint didn't want to distract him from his work, but he couldn't think of anyone better to query about appropriate educational avenues.

"That depends. What kind of education do you want him to have?"

"That's another good question." A boarding school, a day academy, a private tutor? Where? So many questions but they had to settle on a few basics first. "Cassie has begun his schooling, sharing what she knows with him. I think we'd want to let him progress as far as his intellect will allow."

"You might start with locating a tutor to assess his propensity for learning then."

Flint nodded, considering the idea. "I suppose I could

inquire in town. Perhaps my father might even know of someone qualified."

"I have another idea." Daniel selected a nail from his work belt pouch. "You could ask me to teach him."

Flummoxed at his own oversight, Flint could only stare at Daniel. He'd not thought to ask him before. He'd been so sure the brothers would visit and move on he hadn't wrapped his head around the concept they'd linger in the vicinity. "My apologies. I did not think. Would you be interested in doing so?"

"It would put my knowledge to good purpose, so yes, I would." Daniel placed the tip of the nail and quickly hammered it into the board. "Perhaps it will open other doors for tutoring other students."

"You might even start a school of your own if you have enough."

"That's a fine idea." Daniel tapped the hammer on his palm. "I believe it's important to educate the children so they grow up to be decent citizens."

"I will compensate you for your efforts, naturally. We can work out the details later."

"Very good. Well, I should finish up with this skeleton of a wall." Daniel took a step toward the pile of lumber as Teddy came back around it. "There's the new student now."

Teddy stumbled to a halt and gaped at Daniel and then at Flint. "Me?"

"Yes, Mr. Fairhope has agreed to be your tutor. What do you say to that?" The boy's delight shone from his eyes as his gawp turned into a whoop of glee.

"I'll be your best pupil, sir." Teddy beamed at Daniel.

"You'll be my only pupil, at least to begin." Daniel

smiled down at the eager lad. "As soon as I'm finished helping Mr. Hamilton with this addition, we'll begin your studies in earnest."

"Thank you!" Teddy ambled on with his half-empty bucket, still grinning at his good fortune.

The kid had such a good heart. Saving him from following in his father's footsteps flooded satisfaction into Flint's soul. If Teddy had been forced to live in the woods, he'd have wasted his intelligence. Scrabbling for food and succor. For love, for that matter. What did Adam possibly know about how to love someone? Perhaps that's why there was no Mrs. Jacobs. She'd abandoned the man to find love elsewhere. But why leave the boy with him? Some of life's mysteries proved daunting to fathom.

One thing he'd swear for all to hear. Flint would never stop loving Cassie, no matter what life threw at them. Her endearing qualities, her caring and compassion, all brought peace and joy to his heart.

He continued his inspection of the men's work. He stepped over planks and piles of sawdust as he wove through the upright boards. They definitely had made significant progress. But would it all be ready when the caravan of oxen-pulled wagons arrived in mere days? Carrying tired and hungry travelers looking for a place to rest and recover after weeks on the difficult roads. Maybe he could get Cassie to make a hurry-up spellsong to encourage them to work even faster. He chuckled to himself at the silly idea. Better to let them work at a fitting pace rather than a crafted one. But they were running out of time.

Chapter Nine

After the supper rush, Silas sat in the dining room with Cassie while she played a few songs for him on the square piano. She'd asked him to meet her there because she wanted some help with the lyrics. The fact she'd requested his help with the words of her songs immensely pleased him. As if she'd already started to accept him back into the family again. He'd been alone and on his own for so long, coming home felt odd and uncomfortable like a too-tight collar. Perhaps if he continued to feel accepted that collar would loosen more even if he never could remove it. He probably wouldn't be at the inn long enough to find out.

"I think Ma has it right, that when we combine our abilities it increases the power behind them." Cassie rested her hands in her lap after finishing the song. Allegro cocked his head to blink intelligent eyes at him from where he perched on the blanket stand beside the piano.

"Agreed." Did the bird actually understand their conversation? It sure seemed like it did.

She heaved a sigh. "But there's so much I don't know,

Silas. So much I thought I knew and then discovered I didn't know anything." She gave him a wry look. "Our family history is such a mystery."

His childhood wasn't a mystery. He recalled everything perfectly. The two-story brick manor home they lived in. The woods stretching for miles behind his childhood home. The fun he'd had playing outside with his cousin and brothers on those infrequent days when George came over to visit. Going to school in the neighboring town with the other boys in the area. His first kiss from a girl at Sunday school, a bumbling, awkward affair. She'd laughed at him and he stormed away, embarrassed and upset. Then his cousin's drowning, followed by the rupture in the relationship between his parents and the rest of the family. Then everything else fell apart and he was told to hit the road, make a future on his own. That was the past.

"Some of it, true. We know we were happy as children living in that big old house outside of Montgomery. We played with our cousins, swam in the lake down the road every summer. Special days we shared a meal with them, too."

"Way back when we were very young. I don't remember much of those days, to be honest." Cassie played a few chords on the piano and then paused. "It all seems lost in a fog after Pa built this inn. I wonder if that was another of Ma's spells, to obscure my childhood memories from me."

"Why do you say that?" She looked confused, so Silas sat silently while she wrestled with her thoughts. *Take your time. I'm in no hurry.*

She nodded slowly, plinking a key now and again. "Random memories suddenly pop into my brain. Like suddenly remembering we used to know what each other was thinking without having to say it out loud. I'd completely forgotten until you came here."

"I suppose it's possible she did so. Maybe to help you accept living up here." He'd wondered many a time while exiled from the family how his little sister fared. His mother's favorite child if only because Cassie was a girl. "After the argument that broke up the family with Grandmother's death, I suppose."

She stilled and gazed at him. "You know the real reason Ma and Pa moved us up here, don't you? It wasn't Grandma's death but George's. Our aunts blame everything on Pa and Giles for not saving him. Ma said they bound our powers after his death to protect us from our grandfather and aunts trying to use us and our powers toward their own aims."

"I'm sure they thought they were doing the right thing." Even if what they thought and what the fallout entailed remained at odds. The years of isolation, of feeling adrift and not belonging, not being welcomed back into the fold of the family, all combined to encourage his innate desire to wander. To remain aloof and objective rather than becoming entangled in anyone else's affairs. He found objectivity important in order to write most effectively. "She probably really thought she was protecting you by keeping you with her and unaware of your magic."

"Seems likely." She banged on the keyboard with both hands, making a jarring chord with a crash on the keys. "Why is she like that?"

Several startled looks aimed their way. "Because that's her way of protecting us, you in particular. She kept you close because she knew how powerful you would become."

"With all of you home, I can tell a difference in not only

the number of abilities but also my strength with each of them." She slanted a look at him. "Imagine what would happen if all five of us combined our powers."

"Or the entire family." He arched a brow at her. "If combining individual powers increases their strength..."

"An explosion of power could be devastating." Her hands froze on the keys. "We must be careful. Aunt Hope and Aunt Faith have vowed to sway me to do dark magic. That's what Giles and Flint have sworn to protect me from, being persuaded by them to do bad things."

His aunts surely had their own clear reasons for pursuing Cassie so relentlessly. Something must have happened that pointed toward her as the answer to a problem or situation. If only he could determine what that something might be. The only person he imagined could answer his questions was Aunt Hope. As the mother of their long-dead cousin, she would likely know the origin of the animosity between the sisters. Perhaps he needed to inquire with her as to the source. But even an evil person had sound reasons for their actions. He simply needed to discover what her reasons might be.

"I don't think they see it that way." Silas paused to mull over what he wanted to say. To phrase his observation to reflect his emerging thought. "I think they really do want what is best for you and in their view that is to join with them to increase your power along with theirs."

"Why would you say that?" She aimed wide eyes at him. "You think they want to *help* me?"

"We know when we come together we bolster each other's abilities. Ma even said it herself, we're stronger together." He tapped a finger on his chin. "So they are striving to help you see that, by joining forces, you and they will be stronger."

If only they'd want to work together for good.

Good and bad are relative to the situation and the people involved, sis.

There is a gang of men who seem to think they are doing good but we don't believe so. Is that what you mean?

Indeed. That wasn't the first time he'd heard of the fears they held toward the supposed gang. Perhaps he needed to look into them more closely, literally feel them out as to their intentions. Only then could he decide for himself whether they might pose a threat.

She played the refrain of the song she'd finished a few minutes earlier. Its light-hearted tone served as a counterpoint to her serious contemplation. He listened, waiting while she worked out a plan in her mind. Until she ended the piece with a little flourish and gazed at him.

I know what I need to do. Thank you.

Let me know if I can help. "It's not going to be easy, you know."

Despite all of the uncertainties flowing around the inn, he knew one thing with certainty. It was a very good thing he'd made the effort to come to see his sister. She was going to need everyone's help to keep her new aim true.

After supper, Silas retreated outside to the back porch of the inn with a steaming mug of coffee and a plate of cake. He intended to grab a few minutes to relish the fine supper he'd just consumed and enjoy the sweet cake and strong coffee to wash it all down. He pushed through the side door and made his way down the covered passage to the set of table and chairs on the porch facing the foothills. But when he turned the corner, preparing to set down his treat, he found the seats occupied by his aunts.

Faith startled but recovered in a flash of ire-filled eyes. Malachi curled at her feet, studying him with cold, unblinking eyes. "Good evening, Silas."

"Evening to you both." He lifted his plate to indicate his innocent intention. "Thought I'd enjoy my dessert out here but I see you had a similar idea. So I'll..."

"Join us, Silas. We haven't had much chance to talk with you." Hope motioned to the railing of the porch with a flick of her wrist. "If you don't mind using the railing as a seat, that is."

He hesitated for only a second before nodding once. He may as well take the gift of an opportunity to see what more he could learn about Hope's feelings on the death of his cousin and its influence on everything that followed. "I don't mind at all."

He rested his mug on the railing and lifted the fork to spear a bite of white cake with creamy frosting. He swallowed and then felt the curious regard of his aunts. Like they wanted him to start the conversation so they could learn his motives. Not likely. He delayed with a sip of coffee, marshalling his thoughts as the hot liquid flowed down his throat. Where to begin?

"Are you enjoying your visit?" He cringed at the inane question popping from his mouth. A typical opener but still, they obviously had their own agenda for their stay. "I mean, with all of us finding our way here it's becoming a bit...crowded."

"I've never held anything against you boys, you must know that." Hope regarded him with reserved caution. "I have missed watching you grow up into such fine men. I understand you became something of a renowned writer. Good for you."

"I've done all right." He'd learned how to broach touchy subjects in his years interviewing people from all walks of life. But this particular topic could be the stickiest one to approach. "I would like to convey my condolences on the death of my cousin George. Something that when I was a boy never occurred to my youthful brain. I have thought of him often."

Hope blinked rapidly for a moment and then calmed. "Thank you. I miss him daily. He's never far from my thoughts. What kind of man would he have grown up to be? It's a sorrowful musing."

"I never really understood what happened that day. Would you mind very much telling me?"

He stabbed another bite of cake, plunking it into his mouth. Waited for his aunt to press her lips tight and swallow hard.

"Well, it happened a long time ago when you were but a boy, so it's not surprising you wouldn't recall." Hope sipped her steaming beverage, glancing warily at Faith. "I don't know that it will do any good to dredge up all of that with you, though. But thank you for remembering him."

She didn't want to dredge up the past, relive all the pain and grief. But Silas had to press for more. He'd prod gently but persistently until he revealed the truth of those past events.

"Cassie mentioned something about my pa and Giles were there at the time." He left the opening, hoping his aunt would take the lead and follow it.

Hope set her cup down on the saucer on the table. "That I have not forgotten. I blame them for George's demise. They—"

"Sister, dear, it's getting chilly." Faith wrapped her shawl tighter about her shoulders to emphasize her point. "You'll catch cold. We should go in."

"But, Faith, we're having such a nice chat with our nephew." Hope indicated Silas with a tilt of her head. "You'll be fine out here a few more minutes, surely."

"I think not. Come, we shall retire now." Faith stood, her cat lurching to its feet. "It's for the best."

"Very well. I am tired." Hope heaved a sigh and slowly stood. "Besides I wouldn't want to bore you with my grievances on such a lovely evening. Good night, Silas. Enjoy your refreshments."

"Good night." What more could he say?

He reached out to them to sense their emotions as they strolled arm-in-arm away through the passage. Hope's weariness and sorrow met his senses, followed closely by a rush of concern and caution from Faith. Odd. It wasn't her son who had died, so why would she desire to end the conversation at that particular juncture? He settled on Aunt Hope's vacated chair and continued eating his cake, one small bite at a time and sipped his lukewarm coffee as he stared at the darkening sky above the sable foothills. Faith seemed harder to fathom than he'd anticipated, but why?

"Do you see that pile?" Cassie led Giles into the parlor the next afternoon. She carried several pairs of trousers and two shirts in her arms, crossing the room to drop them on top of the accusing pile. "It grows every day. I don't know what I'll do come the new year when I need to be out in the garden."

Giles closed the door behind him and surveyed the room as he paced toward her. "Things have a way of working out the way they should. I wouldn't worry about it for now."

She spun around to observe his approach, noting both his careful scan of every corner of the room and the simmering concern behind the easy smile on his face. Her brother could hide from the rest of the world, but she detected the truth and concern underneath the composed expression on his features. Her chest swelled with pride and love for the burly man halting in front of her. The articles of clothing cried silently for her attention. "It's nearing two feet tall and the customers want a quick turnaround since many of them are only here for a night or two." She gripped her hips and shook her head. "Nothing for it but to get started, I suppose."

"You do that and I'll go ask Matt for a tray of tea and cakes. Something to give you the strength to tackle your task. Yes?" Giles tilted his head a bit to one side as he waited for her response.

"Why not. It'll give me an excuse to take a small break between stitches."

"I'll only be a minute. Stay inside where you're safe." Giles spun around and then marched back out the door, his booted steps thudding away into silence.

With a huge sigh, Cassie took her seat and lifted the next item, a ripped pocket on a pair of maroon trousers. She quickly chose an appropriate color and threaded a needle. Using efficient motions she closed the hole in the bottom of the pocket, her thoughts drifting to a new dress pattern she intended to fashion.

The front door crashed open, making her jump from her

seat, clutching the clothing to her chest as she whirled around. A tall man dressed all in black with a mask over his face stalked toward her, the glint of a silver bladed knife in his hand. Fear flashed through her, lightning across dark storm clouds of panic. She mentally called for Giles even as she moved behind the chair.

"What do you want?" The chair didn't provide much of a deterrent. She dashed around and behind the back side of the huge dining table, her thoughts scattered and panicked.

"You won't live to find out, witch." The harsh voice and threatening posture of her assailant ripped through the air.

She mentally reached out to Giles and Silas, begging for their help. She needed to delay until one or more arrived. She started to take a quick inventory of her options, but the man raced around the table fluid as a cat and lunged at her, the tip of the knife grazing her wrist. She gasped and ran to the front of the room to put the large doll's house between them. She had to think, but with him chasing her, that proved impossible. He came at her again, and this time she didn't think just reacted. She sent out a mental blast to keep away from her, leave her alone. He kept coming, one menacing step after the next, so she tried again, concentrating on the message with all her magical might. He faltered, stumbled, at the same moment Giles burst into the room from the covered passage and thundered toward the intruder.

The man took one look at the furious, charging bull of a man and fled out the front door. Giles went after him, but the would-be killer had disappeared as quickly as he'd appeared. Silas raced up to Giles on the front porch, scouring the area without locating the man. Then they hurried back inside before they closed and barred the door.

Cassie sat trembling on a cushioned chair by the fireplace, staring at her brothers, chilled through from the close call. Although afraid, she'd done what she could to protect herself. What did the man want, other than to harm her? Or kill her. She shivered as she imagined how her ma must have felt when attacked. Somehow this felt more personal. The assailant didn't ask for money or jewels or, well, anything. Just her.

"Are you all right, Cassie? Did he hurt you?" Giles strode to her side, scanning her from head to toe, pausing to lift her left wrist. "He nicked you."

She looked where his gazed fixated on the thin trail of blood drying at the back of her wrist. "It doesn't hurt much at least. But, Giles, what just happened? I don't understand."

"I think I do. I should have anticipated this would happen." Giles squatted down in front of her, searching her eyes. "You're being watched, sis. The timing was too perfect for it to be a coincidence."

"I'm a target, aren't I? Like those other poor women."

"I'm afraid so."

"Good thing you called us." Silas sat on a nearby cushioned chair. "Another moment and you might not have been here to tell us your side of the story."

"I-I didn't know what to do at first. Then when he came closer and more threatening, I simply reacted with a mental push to stop him." She shuddered as she relived the intent in the evil man's eyes. "I don't know who he is, but he had hard blue eyes. I'll never forget the look he gave me when he came at me the last time. Right before you came in."

"I'm really glad you're safe and sound." Silas clasped his hands between his knees as he leaned forward to regard

Cassie. "We need to work on your defenses. Surely your powers can be honed to give you more tools to defend yourself until one of us can reach you in a crisis."

Indeed she did need better defensive measures. She didn't want to see her brothers so shaken. They needed a plan. A plan in place for how to react to various kinds of threats. But mainly... "I need a protection spellsong. Will you help me?"

Chapter Ten

His legs barely carried him across the passage to the inn and an ale. Silas stalked into the dining room and went straight to the bar. Flint was nowhere in sight so he slipped behind, grabbed a mug, and splashed cool amber liquid into it, uncaring if he slopped some onto the counter.

Without taking a seat, he gulped down the refreshing beverage. He plonked the mug on the counter and dragged a palm across his lips. Steadier, he turned to survey who else might be in the room. A few men in the back corner, a family by the fireplace, and his aunts in their accustomed seats close to the piano in the front corner. They seemed at ease. Did they know about Cassie's attack? If not, they should. The looks on their faces and their emotional reaction to the news would be enlightening. He dragged in a fortifying breath as he hurried across the room toward them.

"Aunt Hope and Aunt Faith, I'm glad to find you here." He hauled out a chair and sat down, afraid his legs would fail him. His reaction to his sister's near miss proved far stronger than he would ever have expected. The brute tried to kill his gentle, loving sister. He swallowed the knot of fear gripping his throat. "Are you aware of what has just transpired in the parlor?"

Hope arched a haughty brow at him. "I'm sure you're about to tell us since we have no idea."

He reached out to them, sensed only their curiosity about the mystery he'd presented them. No glee or even concern. Faith tilted her head but kept her expression somber. They didn't know. He relaxed, realizing he'd wrongly suspected their involvement with the killers. Which of course was patently ridiculous. He mentally shook himself. They were family, not killers. Took a calming breath and let it out slowly.

"Cassie was nearly killed."

"Oh no!" Hope jumped to her feet, a hand at her throat. "Is she all right?"

Faith also gained her feet, bracing her fingertips on the table. "We should go to her."

"Please, I didn't mean to unduly alarm you. Just inform you. Giles is with her. She's fine." Silas was not. He stood but kept a fist on the table to steady himself. The trembling had lessened but it would be a few more minutes before the rush of fear on her behalf left his system. "While I have a minute of your time, please let me apologize for my abrupt question the other evening. I shouldn't have raised such a sensitive topic without some little warning."

Faith stiffened, her fingers tensing on the table. "Indeed. Your prying was inappropriate and gauche."

"Now Faith, it's fine. Silas was a boy and only saw things through his naïve eyes." Hope lowered her hand to press her stomach. "He couldn't know his father put the idea of deceiving the rest of the family into our sister's head. Nor that she relished the deception."

The aunts' conviction as to his parents' actions, however obscurely referred to, flowed into his core. "I'm unclear what you are referring to. Would you care to explain?"

"We'll have plenty of time later to converse while we're all here." Hope flashed a look at her sister and then grimly met Silas' gaze. "Right now, I want to see my niece for myself and make certain she is indeed all right."

"I assure you she is safe." Thanks to Giles barreling into the room. By the time Silas had responded the would-be killer had fled. Faith's dark look gave Silas a moment of doubt. What did her foreboding expression portend? "If you're in doubt, I'll happily escort you there to see Cassie for yourself, safe and sound."

Flint sauntered up to the table carrying a tray ladened with clean drinkware. His brow wrinkled as he peered at the concerned faces. "Is something the matter with Cassie?"

Silas nodded once as he raised his inner defenses against Flint's response to his next statement. "She was attacked."

No, it couldn't be. Flint raced to the parlor, heart in his throat as he careered from the dining room across the covered passage to burst through the parlor door. "Cassie?"

"Here." Arms wrapped around her waist, she sat on a chair by the snapping fire, Allegro perched on her shoulder. "Calm down. I'm all right."

A swift perusal told him otherwise. He slowed his pace nonetheless and approached her cautiously, Silas trailing behind him. She trembled but not violently. Her slight frown hinted at lingering shock. The dastardly rogue terrified his woman. A swell of protective love filled his chest as he pinned Giles with his murderous gaze. "Is she?"

Giles gained his feet. "She's unharmed, just shaken up."

"She's fortunate we were all nearby." Abram drummed fingers on his kneecap. "I saw Silas dashing across the yard and figured something was up. Then that masked man fleeing from Giles' wrath. Quite the sight, I assure you."

"I got here as fast as I could but too late." Silas sidled around Flint and paced in front of the blazing fireplace, the flickering light silhouetting his rigid frame. "Our ability to talk silently to each other is what saved her. Giles was close enough to scare him away."

"Her attacker didn't count on our mental connection." Giles folded his arms, muscles evident beneath his strained shirt. "But he was waiting for his chance."

A sliver of ice wedged in Flint's heart. "Meaning what exactly?"

"I think it's fairly obvious. She's being watched." Daniel glanced from Flint to Giles. "What's your assessment?"

"He attacked the moment I left the room, so I must agree." Giles tapped a fist on his elbow as he glowered at Flint. "She's being targeted."

Flint swallowed hard and moved to stand beside Cassie. He clasped her shoulders in both of his hands, refraining with an effort from grabbing her tightly. His gut wanted him to whisk her off someplace far away but her brothers studied him with confidence in their steady gazes. He dragged his worried eyes around the group. "Do you promise she'll be safe here?"

Silas stopped pacing to face Flint directly. "We all came here for that express purpose. To ensure our sister was safe and living in a good situation. Which we know now she is not, so we'll do all we can to change that situation. Right, guys?"

Heads nodded around the group, lips pressed into committed lines. Flint acknowledged their resolve and then squeezed Cassie's shoulders. "I know Giles will stay close, Cassie, and the rest will back him up, but I'd still feel better if your father were home. There's greater safety in numbers when under attack."

"Pa will come home soon and help put an end to all of this. I'm all right." She twisted to look up at him, a glimmer of a smile returning to her eyes. "Please don't overreact. I'm surrounded now with manly protection. I don't know that more is needed."

"I want someone with you at all times, please?" Would she resist yet again when he asked that she have a lookout, a guard, a companion? Anything to thwart future attempts to harm his precious love. "I'm distraught for your safety after such a brazen attack."

She rested a hand on his left one, still clasping her shoulder. "With all of my brothers here, and you, and all the others around, surely I'll be safe."

He tensed, reflexively gripping her shoulder. What if one of those "others" turned out to be the culprit? Someone on the premises with a role to play around the inn and thus his presence would not be suspicious. "And yet you were not. Please, Cassie, take sensible precautions by not being alone again."

"He's right, sister." Silas stopped in front of her, his expression solemn and concerned. "That man didn't attack until you were alone. We'll take turns to make sure that doesn't happen again until this man is caught."

"Or men." Flint cringed. "I still think there's more than

one person responsible for the killings."

"The 'Gang'?" Giles huffed and dropped his hands to slide into his front pockets. "I agree. But the Sheriff doesn't want us getting involved."

"Too late." Abram shifted in his seat, smoothing a trouser leg with one hand. "We're already neck deep."

"If only she could go somewhere else, somewhere safe," Daniel mused.

"If only." Flint could take her into town to stay with his parents, but he suspected as long as she stayed in the general vicinity her life remained in danger. "We need to catch them. Then this nightmare will end."

"And we'll only have to worry about our aunts." Cassie gave his hand a brief squeeze and then stood. "I don't know about you, but I have work to do. Silas, will you shadow me this afternoon? We can talk about the spellsong while I take care of a few other tasks."

Silas offered his elbow. "I'm all yours, sis."

She wrapped her hand around his bent arm. "Thank you."

They strode briskly out of the room, her brothers trailing after. Flint remained rooted to the spot, his mind awhirl with possible suspects. He didn't want to contemplate the awful truth swirling through his head.

Chapter Eleven

Later that evening, Silas heard guitar music drifting into the inn from the front porch. He strolled outside to investigate and found Giles strumming gently on the strings, his gaze distant. He paused to peruse the landscape before him, the white crushed rock practically glowing in the moonlight, the surrounding forest a dark perimeter. The dogs lay nearby, their eyes watching him but ears quivering with the sound of the music filling the twilight air.

A peaceful end to a strenuous day. The quiet evening seemed at odds with the earlier tension and terror. Cassie's life in danger. Knowing someone wanted her dead brought his perspective and priorities into clear purpose. He couldn't depart until she was safe from harm.

The music paused as Giles looked up at him. "Is Cassie all right?"

"She's with Flint inside." Silas crossed in front of Giles to claim the other empty chair. "I needed some air and heard you playing."

"It's a nice evening for sitting out here." Giles ran his fingers down the six strings. "And to think."

"Anything in particular on your mind?" The dogs rested their noses on their paws, a sure sign all was quiet and peaceful. If only Silas felt that way inside.

A few more chords sounded before Giles sighed. "I hadn't expected any of this when I came here. Everything is changed and unsettled."

"I know. Somehow it seems to have started with our cousin's death. I don't understand how, but all roads lead back to that event in one way or another."

"George. Yes, his name keeps coming up." Giles picked through a series of notes, the sweet melody a contrast to the topic of their discourse. "I hadn't thought about him much until July but now I can't stop thinking about what happened. Or rather, what should have happened and didn't."

Silas felt the confusion and dismay from his older brother but kept his gaze averted. "Care to elaborate?"

Giles strummed for a moment before continuing. "I saw him dive into the lake. Why I have no idea. We'd told him not to, it wasn't deep enough, but instead of jumping off the rope swing he twisted into a dive. When he surfaced, I could tell something was wrong."

Grief swelled in Giles' core, sharp and bitter followed by a wave of remorse. Silas shielded himself but left enough opening to monitor his brother's well-being. "What happened, Giles?"

"I ran into the water. I don't know exactly what I was going to do, but I had to try something." He drummed his fingers on the gleaming body of the guitar. "Only Pa stopped me."

"He what?" Frowning, Silas leaned forward to peer at his brother. "Why?"

"He struggled to hold me back. I almost got away but he started chanting something, probably a spell of some kind now I think about it. Back then he was far stronger than me and stopped me. We wrestled for a minute until he pulled me out of the water with him and told me to go on home. I looked at George but he wasn't moving and Pa was very angry. So I stomped away and called to the rest of you to come on home and left."

"What did Pa do?" Silas stared at him, but actually replayed the moments Giles described in his mind's eye. "I only vaguely remember any of this."

The hot summer day had started like so many others. A hike to the lake and a day spent playing in the water. A picnic lunch beneath the weeping willows. Starkly blue skies above the blue water, weeping willows gracefully surrounding the pool. Idyllic for a young boy's life. Until the shouting and scuffling.

"He carried George's body back to his mother's house before he came home. Ma was distraught and hysterical. Pa had to give her something from a small vial to calm her down." Giles shook his head, his hands gripping the guitar. "Ma went to Aunt Hope's to see what she could do, but she came back even more upset. That's when everything started to change."

"Aunt Hope said something about their deception began with George's death." Silas thumped his fingers on his knee. He recalled the bitterness his aunts had experienced at the memory of George's death and the aftermath. "That's when Ma bound our powers."

The story slowly became clearer to Silas, the more he unearthed with his questions and the answers they prompted. Still, like any good riddle, it was taking some unexpected turns. Meaning he needed to probe even further to locate the beating heart of the tragic story's truth.

The next morning, Cassie went into the dining room in search of Silas. She found him seated at the bar sipping hot, creamy tea, Flint wiping the counter with a cloth. The droop of Silas' shoulders as he leaned on the counter bespoke the tiredness she sensed emanating from him. Poor man. Little did he anticipate he'd be put to manual labor when he arrived. Chuckling to herself, she strode over to stand beside him.

"How are you doing?" She slid onto the seat. "You've been busy since you arrived."

He dabbed his mouth with a napkin. "Been pondering writing a family history based on the materials upstairs. Could be enlightening."

"Or revealing. I'm interested in what you make of all those papers and books up there."

What would he find within the pages and pages of the books and papers? With good fortune he'd answer many unspoken questions she harbored in her heart. Ones she dared not ponder long because she feared the answers wouldn't be the ones she hoped for. Knowing those answers might change everything. For her.

"Here you go, darling." Flint handed her a glass of apple cider to quench her thirst.

Surprised from her thoughts, she accepted the beverage with a smile. "You know me so well."

"I'm looking forward to getting to know you even better over the rest of our lives." Flint winked at her and then turned to talk to Isaac about a drink order.

She sipped the tartly sweet beverage and then shot a sidelong look at her brother. "When you're finished, will you go with me to talk to Matt about the party menu? I don't want to go alone. Not after what happened."

"Certainly." Silas tossed back the remains of his tea and then pushed away from the bar. "I'm ready."

She swallowed more of the cider and then headed toward the kitchen, Silas beside her. The menu must excel any other over the past months. If she stretched Matt's mind about possibilities, the results should measure up to the quality she envisioned. The perfect way to welcome not only their guests for the celebration but also her family. She wanted her pa to be proud of her. To prove to him she'd be a good wife but also a good housekeeper. Most importantly, to demonstrate her readiness to marry Flint. Would he take to her suggestions? Concerns flowed through her as they made their way from the dining room and through the swinging kitchen door. She paused inside to appreciate the efficient activity within.

How many times had she come through that door to find Sheridan standing on the far side of the table where Matt currently worked, butcher knife flashing in the firelight? Cutting up a haunch of deer to make a stew or made-dish of some delicious variety. Tears smarted her eyes. How she missed Sheridan's quiet, comforting counsel. Soon he would come home along with his wife and son and Cassie's pa. A new-to-her aunt and uncle as well. Times had surely changed since her birthday back in July. So much had transpired she found it hard to fathom.

"Hey, Cassie, what can I do for you?" Matt laid down the knife and wiped his hands on the half apron tied about his midriff.

Blinking out of her reverie, Cassie hurried forward. "I wanted to talk to you about the menu for the gathering on Allhallows."

Silas moved to the sideboard, plucking an apple from a bowl to munch on.

"Of course." Matt sidled around the table to shake hands with Silas. "Good to see you again, Mr. Fairhope."

"And you, Mr. Simmons." Silas nodded solemnly at the man, holding the bitten apple at his side. "I've enjoyed your many delicious meals, everything from breakfast to supper. Thank you."

Cassie flashed a smile at her brother's respect for the other man filling in for Sheridan. *I think you've made his day.*

I'm just relaying my appreciation for a job well executed.

I love you.

And I you.

"Thank you, sir. I am grateful." Matt released Silas' hand and then met Cassie's inquisitive gaze. "I heard about the attempt on your life, miss. Are you sure you're not harmed?"

"I'm perfectly all right. Thank you for asking." His concern was indeed touching. Especially considering his own family remained out on the difficult and dangerous roads. He must worry for their safety and well-being. "Are you excited about your parents and brother arriving in a few days?"

"Yes, miss. I only hope they don't meet with trouble." His brown eyes clouded for a moment before he drew in a breath. "I know they'll take care but I can't help but be concerned."

"Pa said they'd be here soon, so we'll have to keep an eye out for their arrival. What's the first thing you want to do when your father arrives?"

"Ask him his opinion on some menu changes before we present them to Flint, or I suppose your father for approval." He opened his mouth to say something more but hesitated. Then he squared his shoulders. "And his opinion on possibly opening my own place."

Matt's comment provoked a new consideration. When her pa came back, Flint would no longer need to be innkeeper in his place. What would he do then? Would her pa want him to stay on or send him back to town? While she'd be required to stay at the inn until they married. The thought of him leaving, of not seeing him daily, shook her composure. She'd come to rely on his stalwart belief in her even if he doubted himself at times. When the oxen-pulled wagons arrived more things would change. How exactly? She must ensure proper arrangements were made for the upcoming event to further demonstrate her management skills. After all, she couldn't rely on magical abilities for every aspect of her life..

"If you're interested in having your own tavern or inn, then you should see what it would take. I'm sure it would be grand. In the meantime, I hope you haven't settled on the menu for Allhallows." She focused on him until she felt the weight of the kitchen maids' appraisal and then struggled to keep her attention on the cook. Why were they staring at her so? "I'd like to make a few suggestions."

"I've been thinking about what to include that would be fittin'." Matt hefted the knife, the blade glinting as he resumed cutting the meat into chunks.

"With the cooler temperatures, I'm thinking some hearty

soups and stews." Cassie sensed interest but not from the man in front of her. She swept her gaze around the room as the weight of two pairs of eyes increased and then spotted Myrtle and Meg working at the sideboard as usual. But their appearance was anything but usual. She frowned as she addressed Matt. "Chicken stew and maybe sweet potato soup."

"Those seem rather common. What if we tried some more interesting dishes since it's a celebration?" Matt tapped a forefinger against his chin. "Stuffed pork roast and parsley potatoes with creamed asparagus and hot rolls?"

"Deal me in for that dinner." Silas crunched into the apple, bobbing his head with enthusiasm.

The combination did make her mouth water. The savory flavors of roasted pork with the buttery herbed potatoes, tender asparagus with a heavy cream sauce drizzled over the stems, along with piping hot yeast rolls. Who wouldn't be tempted by such fare? "You've some wonderful ideas, Matt. This time of year it's easy to find deer, so maybe some venison creation?"

As she spoke, she sensed more than witnessed a silent exchange between the two scullery maids. She surreptitiously glanced at the sisters. Something seemed different with them. But what? They dressed as always in workaday pastel cotton dresses, a bibbed white apron protecting the skirts. Hair pulled back out of their way. She reached out to sample their emotions and realized what had changed. Their confidence soared, evidenced by their stature straight and sure, and their overall appearance no longer plain, instead suffused with energy and light. But their eyes stunned her with their colorful orbs unlike any others she'd seen. Having identified the physical and emotional changes, she wanted to know the source. The last time she'd seen them, a few days before, they'd not looked anything like the vibrant young women keeping an eye on her.

"Do you think folks would enjoy that, miss?"

Startled out of her musings and back to the present conversation, she pasted a rueful smile on her lips. "I'm sorry, Matt, I was distracted. What were you saying?"

The man regarded her for a split second before glancing at the two maids. His brows rose as he blinked slowly several times before meeting Cassie's gaze again. "I...I could make some chicken and dumplings with peas and carrots for those who might want something lighter. Do you think that would be good?"

Matt's confusion matched her own after he'd really seen the two young women, two long-time fixtures of the kitchen who had transformed from gray haired "old" ladies into alluring and capable young women. No wonder Cassie hadn't noticed before, used to them being there at the fringes without interacting, without saying much of anything. She'd thought them middle-aged but now they seemed to be her age. Something had definitely happened to them. She would find out, and soon.

"Yes, that sounds fine." She avoided looking at the maids by catching Silas' eye. "I think we're done here." For now.

The scrape of the key in the attic door seemed loud later that morning. Silas eased into the shadowy room, his candle a flickering defense. Pocketing the key, he crossed to light the lamp on the table by the window. He turned up the flame to brighten the room as much as possible to look around, take note of the contents of his mother's private sanctuary. The room contained her most treasured belongings, not only family heirlooms. Pictures, books, and furnishings which she chose with care. Thus the attic reflected not his mother but the inner person, her true self.

He closed his eyes to let his senses absorb the atmosphere of the space. A sense of contentment, or peace, pervaded. Interwoven threads of lingering sadness, flashes of fear, and wary anxiety completed the emotional tapestry of his mother's attic. Opening his eyes, he continued his evaluation, his gaze alighting on the blanket draped over the back of the chair by the table where the lamp merrily blazed. Compelled to touch it, he strode over to clutch it in one hand.

A jolt of emotional memory had him grabbing the chair to steady himself. He hugged the blanket to his chest, the memories coming fast and furious into his mind. She'd wrapped herself in the soft fibers while seated in the carriage on the way from southern Alabama. Her mother's gift. The last one. Crocheted with love in every stitch. He stared at the blanket for a long moment, his ma's deep sadness at the loss of her mother reverberating in his soul, then laid it back over the chair. He slowly drew in a breath and then just as slowly released it. He couldn't let himself become entangled with the emotional baggage each article he touched carried. He had work to do and not much time to do it.

Cassie had practically thrown the set of keys at him so he could explore and scrutinize the many papers and letters secreted within the old trunk. Knowing his father would arrive in mere days and occupy the abandoned bedroom below made his errand all the more urgent. Pa would control the keys and access to his mother's attic and then how would Silas ever gather the information he needed? He pulled a small battered notebook and pencil from his coat pocket, opening it to be ready to receive any notes he needed to jot down, and laid it on the lid of a neighboring trunk.

He lifted the lid of the repository of the family's past and started with the first paper to come to hand. He skimmed the articles on the several pages of the *Montgomery Times* of October 30, 1817. Nothing of interest. New hat fashions. The day and time of a meeting to organize a local fire department. Then he frowned at the underlined headline of an article, a bold underscore marking it important, buried in the back of the paper: MYSTERY MAN FOUND SCORCHED; LEFT FOR DEAD. After some poking around, the authorities determined the man in question was one Robert Covington, a suspicious enough fellow on the best of days. Known to have made many enemies during his life in the area, nobody seemed overly surprised to find him dead. Speculation ran rampant as to who had finally succeeded in ridding the region of Covington's bad influence. The coroner couldn't explain the cause of death based on his injuries, the marks left all over his body appeared as if Zeus had been tossing lightning bolts at him. Long, black sooty marks all over his head and torso hinted at some form of hot substance being shot at him. But one thing was vastly clear. Whoever had killed Covington had vented their wrath on the man using an unknown weapon. Legends had grown surrounding the possible scenarios for his death as a result. Silas laid the paper aside. Odd and intriguing. But who exactly was the man? And what had he done to provoke such antagonism?

The next newspaper, a *Huntsville Ledger* from June 5, 1815, included a starred story of how Reginald Fairhope had broken ground on building a new roadside inn along Winchester Road. At the base of the Fury Falls and its accompanying mineral springs, the inn would accommodate up to twenty overnight guests and seat upwards of one hundred for dinner. The reporter glossed over the reasons for choosing the site, but did briefly mention the previous owner had been anxious to sell and move for personal reasons. Probably had sick relatives back east, the writer speculated. Silas smirked at the page, other possibilities floating through his mind, as he placed it on top of the other.

Next came another article from the *Montgomery Times*, this time about the accidental death of one Charity Miller Covington at her home outside of the city on Valentine's Day, 1814. Another Covington dying under mysterious circumstances. He perused the few short paragraphs detailing the fact she'd been home with her daughters when something in the kitchen exploded and caught fire, killing the mother instantly. The kitchen had burned so hot and fast the cause of the explosion could not be determined. The three girls were fortunate to be alive.

Silas stared at the paper for countless minutes, his mind reeling. Covington. Two in under four years, both dying under inexplicable circumstances. What were the odds of such occurring? Pretty damn slim, certainly. He lifted the other *Times* and reread the short article, a shiver trickling down his back when he read that the man had been survived by three daughters, but preceded in death by his wife, Charity. Even less likely they'd be husband and wife and die under not only mysterious but violent circumstances. He made quick notes of the details, sensing the specific facts formed the kernel of the tale he needed to tell.

Three girls, too. The woman's name was Charity. Another shiver rocked his shoulders. Her daughters could very well be Hope, Faith, and Mercy, then. All biblical concepts applied to sweet young girls, who in turn became witches. He stared at the two papers in his hand, certainty filling his soul. If the surviving daughters included his mother, then the two dead Covingtons were his grandparents.

He pushed to his feet and paced to the bookshelves on the wall. Scanning the titles, he found books covering subjects as wide-ranging as botany, the history of Ireland, a primer in grammar, a tattered copy of a book on mythology and lore, as well as a few maps of the United States, Alabama, and Georgia. One title jumped out at him, though. He pulled *Mixing and Matching Magical Elements* by Marigold Leifwald from the shelf with tentative fingers. He opened the cover to find his mother's name carefully inscribed on the first page, answering in bold strokes the question of ownership. Inside lists of herbs, minerals, gases, and incantations were cross-referenced to later spells and recipes for concoctions and potions. If any doubts lingered in his mind, the tome proved his mother and her family were involved with magic. He replaced the book and surveyed the rest of the cozy retreat from everyday life.

The table and chair were positioned so his mother could read comfortably, either by the light of the oil lamp or the sunlight coming through the window. A thick carpet on the floor comforted her feet and dispelled the chill in the air.

The Franklin stove also served to keep the room warm and cozy on winter days. As he slowly, inch by inch, pivoted to drink in his surroundings, he could easily imagine his mother spending many hours of quiet and solitude within its four walls. Keeping her own secrets regarding her family's witchy ways.

"Silas, what are you doing in here?" Mercy shimmered abruptly into the room beside him. "You should have asked me."

He couldn't help the hop of surprise but covered it with a pair of fingers touched to his brow. "Ma, I didn't expect you."

"In my own attic?" Mercy drifted a few inches away so she could scowl at him. "How stupid do you think I am?"

"I have never questioned your intelligence. But you did say you saved these papers for me. So, you've already essentially given me permission to read them." Silas spotted his open notebook and moved to snatch it up, flip it closed, and slide it out of sight. "But to answer your first question, I've decided to write our family history based on what I learn from the papers."

"Write a history of our family?" She shifted side to side with increasing agitation, peering at him through narrowed eyes. "I don't know if that's a good idea, son."

"Why? What's there to be afraid of?" Perhaps her insights and memories would provide a focal point to anchor the core of the story, of his family's past endeavors. "I'd like to interview you. Are you amenable?"

"What if the wrong people get their hands on it?" She shook her head, crossing her arms over her chest. "I don't think you should do a written history. Just read about it, but don't put all the pieces together. Please?"

"I hear you, Mother, but I think we—as in, your children—need to understand where we came from in order to not only protect us from the present threats but to forge a path into our future. That's vital and will ultimately help the family come together again. We deserve to know the truth of what happened." He closed the trunk lid and brushed his hands off before extinguishing the lamp. He strolled to the door, pausing to look back at her still worried countenance. She simply didn't trust him. "It'll be fine. Nothing bad will happen from knowing our past. I promise."

Chapter Twelve

Thanks for talking with me for a minute." The sun cast short shadows around the gazebo. Cassie didn't have much time before she needed to be in the dining room for the luncheon rush. "Take a seat and let's chat, shall we?"

Myrtle flowed regally across the gazebo floor in a lavender cotton dress with a white apron tied around her waist to settle onto the lefthand of the three metal benches arrayed under the vine-covered roof. Her multicolored eyes swirled as she regarded Cassie. "I'm surprised you noticed anything was...different."

Cassie hesitated as Meg went to the center bench and sat down, fluid as a fox disappearing into the brush. And in *her* preferred seat. With a suppressed sigh, Cassie turned to claim the righthand seat, skimming her gaze over the sisters. No point in antagonizing them when she had questions.

Giles took up a position at the base of the steps, his gaze sweeping the area. Allegro cried from on high and soon swooped down to alight on the rail of the gazebo, close to Cassie but on alert as well. Cassie nodded to her familiar, aware he stood on guard alongside her brother. After all, they were away from the sheltering walls of the inn. Exactly where Cassie had been attacked the first time. She still needed that protection spellsong.

Meg studied her with dancing light in her eyes. "Is something on your mind, miss?"

Cassie reached out with her senses to see how they were feeling. Curious, naturally. Confident, too. A deeper probe yielded self-assurance unlike any Cassie had experienced in others. What was the source? Two kitchen maids who once presented as old maids. Living together in the woods not far from the inn. They'd worked at the inn for several years, meek as dormice and about as noticeable. Now they sparkled with animation and verve. Strength and purpose. She'd push acceptance toward them but decided to gauge their reaction to her questions before resorting to her magic.

"Yes, there is something on my mind." Cassie smoothed her calico dress over her knees. "You both seem different somehow. What has happened?"

"Different...how?" Myrtle smiled gently at her, conveying calm and good humor.

Cassie shrugged lightly, clasping her hands in her lap. "It's hard to say. Your hair for one thing. I always thought it was rather gray, but now it looks more like polished silver."

"You noticed. Thank you. I had hoped you would." Myrtle relaxed in her seat, her gentle smile broadening. "I honestly didn't think anyone ever noticed me."

"Of course I noticed you, Myrtle. And Meg." She'd thought of them as grandmotherly types, which apparently was an assumption based solely on their appearance. If she'd bothered to become more acquainted with them as women she'd most likely would have realized her error. Cassie shot a peek at the other sister. "I may not have spoken to you as often as I would have liked, but I did see you both."

"Yes, we know." Meg regarded the big man standing with feet braced apart, eyes roaming the front of the inn, the carriageway, the numerous carriages and coaches traversing to and fro. "I appreciate the fact that you did. So what is on your mind now?"

"We're happy to answer any questions you may have." Myrtle fairly smirked at her, making Cassie blink in surprise. "We wouldn't be here if we didn't want to be. Ask away."

The woman knew something had changed and waited to see just how long it would take for others to notice. A game of sorts. Or a test. The flash of a silent message between them alerted Cassie to a shared secret. Yet another one.

"I think you know already what my questions are, so why don't you just answer them." Cassie tightened her interlaced fingers. "That will save us all some time since we need to get back to work soon."

"Very well. Let's get to the point. My birthday present is what happened." Myrtle glanced at Meg and then back to Cassie. "We found out on my twenty-first birthday our true ancestral heritage. The fact that we're the daughters of the beloved elven king and queen of the Willow Forest people, which makes us princesses."

Cassie stared wide-eyed at the sisters. Giles paused in his surveillance to blink slowly at them as well. She reached out and confirmed they spoke the truth. Elves working at the inn. In the kitchen.

"With powers?" Cassie asked, holding her breath until they revealed them.

"Why of course. What would an elf be without any

special faculties?" Meg stood and paced to stare up the dirt trail between the inn and stable, leading up the mountain to the springs and the falls beyond. "I can control water, any liquid actually. And I have clear-knowing, the ability to gather information from those around me. It's been quite interesting learning to not only control but use both powers."

"Control liquid. That's something." Cassie grinned up at her, clasping her fingers more tightly. How would the elf use that capability? To whose benefit? She slid her gaze to Myrtle. "And yours are?"

"I can sense when others with magic are near and I can control objects." Myrtle also stood and moved to take up a position near her sister. "You needn't worry, Miss Fairhope."

"Cassie, please. Go on." Cassie sensed their loyalty, their intent to help not hinder. She relaxed more, Allegro flapping his wings once from his perch nearby in acknowledgement of her change in defensive posture. "I don't understand why you came back to be maids when you know you're princesses and the rest that must go along with that."

"Why, to protect you all here, of course." Myrtle slid a look at Meg and then met Cassie's gaze. "We love working here, love the people."

"Indeed. We love being a part of this growing and thriving inn. We want to do whatever we can. We know something evil is about, something dangerous on the horizon. But can you tell us what we're actually up against?"

"Yes, like why your aunts have shown up again." Myrtle resumed her seat. "I get the impression they're not welcome and yet they stay on without any attempt by anyone to help them on their way. We could facilitate that, if that's what you want."

"More than anything I want them to leave me alone, but not by force." Cassie sank against the bench and shook her head. Allegro made a quick flight hop from the railing to her shoulder, rubbing his head against her neck with consoling affection. "I'd prefer they go of their own accord. I have an idea of how to make that happen but it will take time to work out."

"In the meantime, tell us about what's going on around here." Meg settled on the bench beside her sister, fingers clasping her knees through her pale yellow skirts.

"The short version is all we have time for, I'm afraid." Cassie peered at Giles, waited for his agreement signaled with a dip of his head, and then launched into a quick summary.

She reviewed everything she'd told them. From when Giles became Guardian to when Silas arrived with his wordsmithery talents. Of discovering the vast array of family secrets and their implications. The progression from suspecting John Baker to suspecting the gang. Her aunts' first attempt to take her with them to their current stance of heavy-handed persuasive techniques. Even meeting Allegro for the first time. Had she forgotten anything?

"Now that you know everything, are you sure you want to be part of this mess?"

Myrtle and Meg rose as one and held out a hand to her. "We're honored you'd trust us, Cassie."

Cassie rose and took their hands so they formed a circle within the shade of the gazebo, Allegro balancing easily. "For now, as Flint is fond of saying, the more there are of us to defend the inn and all who work and play here, the better."

Giles folded his arms as he silently observed the three women. Cassie reassured him silently, sending heartfelt thanks for his keen eye, his caring, and merely being nearby as she worked through even more surprising revelations. He responded in kind, assuring her of his constant protection. At a sound from one of the elves, she brought her attention back to the matter at hand.

"We've thought for some time that all wasn't as it seemed." Myrtle squeezed Cassie's hand. "Never fear. We sensed something bad coming but didn't know what. Now we can help."

"Even our mentor, Elswyth, has vowed to assist all she can. She looks more like an elf than either of us, all sparkly and colorful and spritely."

Wait until Flint heard that he'd hired elves to work in the inn's kitchen. Ones who vowed to help defend the people and property against the threats facing everyone and everything. Wait until her pa learned of their presence as well. What might he have to say about them?

"I happily anticipate the pleasure of meeting her." Cassie squeezed their hands and then let go. "Now it's time to get to work before Flint comes in search of us. There's no time like the present to begin working together on a new level, with a new aim. Keeping all of us safe."

After stewing over everything he'd learned and pondering what else he needed to know, Silas went in search of Aunt Hope the next afternoon. Storm clouds covered the sky, a thunderstorm building over the foothills. Was it common for such a storm to threaten in the fall? He didn't know but he suspected the atmosphere sensed his angst and reacted accordingly. In fact, the discussion might be more comfortable outside where they had wide open spaces to host the tense exchange. But not with lightning flashing and thunder rolling closer with each passing minute. He descended the stairs from the second floor of the residence and scanned the family parlor space. He couldn't believe his luck.

Hope sat reading a large black book near the fireplace. Her intent expression showed signs of years of worry and grief. He didn't fathom the depth of her pain, as she guarded her emotions from casual access. He'd need to use his skills to learn more.

"Aunt Hope, I was hoping to find you." Silas stepped onto the painted floor boards and crossed to the conversation grouping by the crackling fire in the large fireplace. Her haughty eyes met his cautious smile. "Shall I ask for a tea tray?"

"Are you planning to stay a spell?" Her smirk confirmed the double entendre of her question. "But, no thank you. I have had my surfeit of tea for the day."

"In that case, may I join you? I have a few questions I'd like to ask you while we have some privacy."

Hope shifted in her seat, smoothing the long maroon skirts of her day dress over her legs. The rounded toes of her black leather shoes peeked from beneath the hem. "I have a few minutes while Faith is napping."

Silas sank onto the armchair opposite his aunt and looked away from the intense appraisal in her hard eyes. Red and blue flames danced with orange and green among the pile of logs. The aroma of freshly baked bread teased his nose, setting his mouth to watering in anticipation of a sumptuous dinner. First, he must make the most of his good fortune to find her alone and willing to speak with him. He forced his gaze to meet hers. Where to start?

"Aunt Hope, I know George's death is at the core of what caused the rift between our families. What I don't understand is how such a tragedy caused so much animosity. Can you enlighten me?"

So many questions waited to be asked. He held his tongue as she wrestled for a time with her response.

"As I've said, Reggie didn't allow Giles to help my son, and then stood by while George died." Hope's eyes glistened with tears begging for release but denied. "How could he?"

"Have you talked to him about that day?"

"I have and he's denied letting him die. He claims the boy was dead when his body surfaced." Hope stared at Silas and then slid her gaze to stare into the fire. "He said there wasn't anything they could have done without exposing the family's secrets to the public."

"George died after his dive into the water then." Silas studied his aunt, sensed her resistance but also a hint of loneliness. He probed more. "You don't blame Mercy, just Reginald?"

Hope flashed a harsh look at him. "I want that man to at least apologize for his role in my son's death. Giles has already, not that I totally blame the boy for his father's actions."

"If he apologizes, will you be willing to put the past behind us? Try to unite the family in peace again?"

Somehow mending the rift in the family became all the more important knowing how much it really would mean for their future happiness. He had no illusions of staying on at the inn, but he hoped to leave knowing he'd made a difference. A good one stemming from his words.

"I don't know. I do know if he never does, then I have no reason to try." She stared at the fire, the popping and hissing echoing the roar of the wind around and the rumble of thunder above the inn. "My precious son is lost to me forever."

"I understand my pa carried George home to you. Is that right?"

"Yes, we buried him in the family cemetery between our houses. Why?"

"No reason. I'm trying to put the pieces together in my head. I assume Aunt Faith was with you when my pa told you about your son's death?"

"Faith?" Hope dragged her gaze from the fire to meet his. "No, I don't recall her being home at the time. I was alone."

Which would make the arrival of her son's dead body in the arms of her brother-in-law all the more tragic and traumatic. No one should face such news without the loving support of family or friends.

"I'm sorry for that, Aunt Hope. It must have been very difficult for you without your sister there." He laid a hand on her wrist for a second. "Where was she?"

"I don't know." She frowned, pursing her lips before pressing them together. "Probably out in the woods in search of some herb."

A flare of longing in her surprised Silas. His aunt had harbored a very slim hope of connecting with Mercy, but the glimmer was fading into oblivion now that she'd passed on. Hope had longed to create a bridge in the family by convincing Cassie to unite with her and Faith but even that dimmed with each passing day and Cassie's aversion to the idea. Still Hope remained determined to find a way to convince her niece to agree to her terms. Another dying wish.

"Well, thank you for clarifying what happened that day." The woman's revelations showed him the importance of his work to write a family history which would shed light on the past. Everyone needed to know who had done what so they could forge a new path for the family. He'd uncovered the surprising fact that George was dead when Giles had struggled with their pa to try to save him. If anyone had seen Giles' superhuman strength at the juncture, the family's other special skills and talents would have eventually come to light. One new major question arose from his conversation with Hope.

Where was Aunt Faith when the drowning occurred?

"Say that again, please." Flint leaned back in his office chair. Tapping the pencil tip on the blotter, he could only stare at Cassie's bemused expression. "I don't believe I heard correctly."

How was it remotely possible? The two gray-haired women seemed innocuous and meek. He'd counted on them to continue to provide their scullery and food preparation assistance. But now how could he ask them to do so? Surely Cassie teased him about the changes to their appearance as well as their heritage. He hadn't noticed any differences, so... He mentally crossed his fingers as he waited for her response.

"Myrtle and Meg Marple are elf princesses." She clasped her fingers on the desk across from him, her eyes dancing with fun. "Isn't that wonderful?"

"Such news is difficult to digest in one swallow." He laid the pencil down and attempted to still his agitated fingers. Giles sat beside Cassie, humor twinkling in his eyes. "My kitchen maids are princesses? I can't quite grasp how that is possible. Why would they choose to work in the kitchen?"

"They didn't know, not until recently. And they've chosen to stay working in the kitchen so they are close by to help us when we need them." Cassie arched one brow at him. "Their elfish abilities will augment ours in some startling ways, too."

She continued to fill him in on everything she'd learned about Meg and Myrtle. Including the meaning behind their names. Meg, or rather Megara, controlled water. Named after one of the Furies, the one who punished those guilty of infidelity, she also gleaned knowledge others couldn't. But Myrtle, whose name represented not only Venus but the myrtle bush which was an ancient symbol of love, controlled any objects she chose. Cassie also pointed out that their physical appearance had changed with their new-found abilities and awareness of their elf parents and the Willow Forest people.

The more he thought about all she'd told him the more he realized how little he'd been paying attention to the people around him. Including his own staff, for goodness sake. Not only had they changed, but he needed to also. Be more aware. Be better informed. Be a better boss and friend as a result.

"What triggered their transformation?" He grabbed up the pencil and wiggled it between thumb and forefinger to relieve the tension the news had wrought.

"Myrtle's coming of age, as far as her parents are

concerned at least." She shrugged as she refolded her fingers. "She turned twenty-one and an elf envoy delivered the surprising news that evening. She had to reach her maturity in order to be trusted with the knowledge of her heritage."

"Where are her parents? Why didn't they bring the news instead of sending someone else?" Such a confusing situation to sort through. The sisters' parents couldn't be bothered with revealing the secret themselves. Leaving it to a third party to reveal the truth of their ancestry. How convenient.

"Well, they died several years ago." Cassie's frown hinted at her discomfort with the topic. "At least they made the necessary arrangements for the girls to learn the truth."

"A magical birthday message, you mean?" Flint tapped the pencil harder. "How did they take the news?"

"They are happy to find out their true natures and all that came with it. They're rich and revered by the Willow Forest people, so they no longer feel invisible." She paused as her eyes twinkled. "Myrtle in particular thought it rather surprising I even observed the change in her. She thought nobody noticed her."

"I shall be sure to pay closer attention." Flint glanced at the Guardian with a question in his gaze. "What's your take on all of this?"

"Having more magical or special creatures around the family can only be a benefit." Giles crossed his arms, relaxing in the creaking chair. "More folks to defend against whatever threats may arise."

"Good point. Having a varied tool box should be useful indeed." Flint dropped the pencil, aggravated at his own disquiet. He should be happy to have more help. "Now what?"

"There's nothing to do about the girls having special abilities except be happy for them." Cassie stood, preparing to return to work to prepare for the dinner rush in a matter of minutes. "Anything else we need to discuss before I go?"

Giles also rose to his feet. "We need a family meeting, including the Marple sisters, to discuss how we can best work together with these new tools in said box."

"Agreed but..." Cassie tapped the wooden desk with her index finger. "Let's do that tomorrow evening. I have a few things I need to attend to before we get everyone together."

"Tomorrow night then. I'll see to it." Flint also gained his feet, scanning the faces of those around him. Feeling like he needed to attend to a few things himself, namely improving how he interacted with others. "For now, let's get to work."

Chapter Thirteen

After his conversation with Aunt Hope, Silas took a few minutes to make some notes in his book. Sometime later he headed to the dining room and a stiff drink. Or at least, something stronger than ale. He strode into the room, noting his aunts seated at their usual table, and barely glanced at the others as he made his way to a seat at the bar. He ignored the looks from the other guests, but he sensed the general convivial mood of the room. He relaxed as he waited for Flint to arrive to pour him a whiskey, not wanting to overstep his welcome again by pouring it himself. He'd been desperate last time and unwilling to wait, but this time he'd adhere to the established boundaries. While he waited, he'd open himself a bit more to the others and see what he could glean from their emotional state.

The guests laughed and talked behind him. Cassie's voice floated through the air, entertaining and encouraging. Turning around, Silas perused the room. All the cloth-covered tables were occupied by men in suits or working attire. Women in fine gowns graced several of the groups.

His aunts observed Cassie's performance with solemn yet pleased expressions. Could he write a story of his family's past which could heal old wounds?

"Ah, Mr. Fairhope, a pleasure to see you today."

"Good day." Silas pivoted to meet the smug grin of John Baker as he slid onto a seat. His attire on this stormy afternoon compromised between his preferred vibrant colors and the necessity of his black overshoes and cloak to protect the refined clothing beneath. Worry and impatience flowed from him as he slid a look at Silas. "How are you, sir?"

"I understand Reginald will be arriving in a few days and I must admit to being relieved of the duty to oversee Flint's job here." John tapped a finger on the counter and then stilled his hand. "He's done a fine job, mind, but I'll be able to focus more closely on my own farms."

"They surely must need your attention." The deep voice of Sterling Nelson vibrated the air as the tall man halted beside John. "You've been here more often than not."

Silas stiffened at the umbrage contained in the man's tone as well as the distrust in his core.

Flint strode quickly behind the bar and poured an ale which he slid toward Sterling. "Mr. Nelson, a pleasure to see you here. Have you met Silas Fairhope?"

"Thank you, my boy. No, I've not had the...pleasure." Sterling scanned the room and then met Silas' gaze. "Are you enjoying yourself?"

Taken aback, Silas stared at the gruff man. "I am, thank you."

"I hope so. Ah, here's Larry." Sterling greeted the waiter with a nod. "Might I trouble you for a bowl of something hot?"

Larry smoothed a white towel over his shoulder. "Of course. I'll be right back with your dinner."

"Very good. You're doing a fine job, sir." Sterling inclined his head to the younger man in appreciation of his efforts.

"Thank you, sir. I enjoy my job here very much and hope to remain as long as possible. I'll be right back with your meal." Larry tipped fingers to his brow as he spun on one heel and marched out of the room to retrieve the older man's dinner.

"That young man has quite a good future here." John watched Larry disappear around the corner before he swung his attention back to Sterling. "I believe we owe you for sending him to the inn."

"Yes, the inn owes me." Sterling traveled his gaze about the room, seeming to avoid John's drooping smile.

Suddenly, Silas was forced to raise his inner defenses when a wave of fear followed by a crash of anger surged through him. He tensed and then forced his shoulders back down before slowly turning around to peruse the room at large. Several groups of working men lingered over a late afternoon meal, hoping to avoid the worst of the downpour outside before they were forced back on the road to their work or homes. No anger stemmed from them. His aunts chatted quietly while keeping their perusal keen about their surroundings, but neither stewed with fear let alone anger. The two men beside him likewise didn't seem to hold any fear, not distinctly, though they were both very guarded as to their emotions. So who was it he sensed?

Cassie went in search of her aunts. Giles trailed after her, keeping her in sight but back far enough to survey the surroundings. Her shadow. There to protect her from anything which might arise. She blew out her anxiety in a long exhale. The family meeting could be pivotal in bringing everyone together, in sorting out who could use which weapons in defense of the family. She grabbed the door latch to go into the inn side, thinking her aunts might be in the dining room, and hesitated. She reached out to ascertain her aunts whereabouts. She let go of the latch and turned around to face the direction she'd come. Giles halted several strides away, tilting his head in query. She pressed her lips together. If the entire family were to work together, that included her aunts. Not that they'd likely listen to her.

"I need to talk to Aunt Hope and Aunt Faith before our family meeting." She stepped closer to her solemn brother. "I think I sense them upstairs. Will you wait in the parlor while I go up to their room?"

"Don't be long." Giles pivoted and marched back to the open parlor door, ushering her inside. "Go on then."

She slipped past him and hurried across the room to climb up the stairs. Rapping on the door to her aunts' chamber, she waited as the conversation inside quieted. Then footsteps approached and the door swung open.

"Cassandra. How lovely to see you." Aunt Faith squinted at her while Malachi wound about her ankles. "What brings you to see us?"

"May I have a word with you in the parlor?" The cat sat down and stared at her with its yellow eyes, the swirl of white on its chest the only relief on the ebony feline. She dragged her gaze back to her aunt, sensing unease she'd never detected in her before. Echoes of the quiet conversation she'd interrupted made her wonder what exactly they'd been discussing. From the look on her face, it was a sore topic. But what she had to say couldn't wait. "It's important."

"Who is it?" Aunt Hope called from inside the room.

"Our pretty niece, wanting a word downstairs." Faith opened the door wider so Cassie could see Hope, dressed in a black dress with dark gray edging, supine on the four-poster bed. "Are you willing?"

Cassie gripped the doorframe with one hand. Her aunt took her role as a witch to heart. Why did she shout to the world not to trust her by wearing such obvious witch attire? She may as well carry a straw broom and cackle at the slightest provocation. Cassie suppressed the aggravation simmering in her chest. Focusing on how to convince her aunts to help the rest of them took precedence. Not critiquing her fashion sense. She pasted a smile on her lips.

"I'd really appreciate a few minutes of your time if you're rested." She kept the smile in place, pushing out the desire to accept the request in hopes her aunts could be influenced by her thoughts. "It won't take long, I promise."

Hope stretched and yawned. "Why can't you say whatever it is here and now?"

Her brother's anxiety reached Cassie, tugging on her to return to where he could keep an eye out for her safety. "Giles is waiting for us in the parlor. Please come down as soon as you're ready."

"How cheeky." Faith started to close the door when Hope stopped her with a grunt. Faith cast a sidelong look at her sister. "We're going?"

Hope rolled to one side and sat up to peer at Cassie for several beats. "I suppose. Give me a minute, child."

"Thank you." Cassie walked away from the hot gaze of

Faith. If only Allegro were with her, perhaps she'd feel more settled. As it was, she had Giles to back her up if things became heated between them. She'd make do.

She descended the stairs slowly, her thoughts spinning. Arranging her arguments. Aligning their aims with hers. Or trying to. Finding ways to parallel what they wanted from her to what she needed from them proved difficult. But once she settled on how to go about it, she felt better. Until she started seeking holes in her approach. And identifying too many.

Within a few minutes, her aunts joined her and Giles in the parlor by the snapping flames in the fireplace. She studied her aunts as they claimed chairs by the fire. Giles leaned an elbow on the mantel, surveying the gathering and keeping a watchful eye on the doors.

As much as Cassie longed to avoid the discourse, she took a deep breath and began. "I've asked you here to ask your help. As you know, Pa is on his way and should arrive any day now. He's bringing with him one of his sisters and one of his brothers, family I haven't met but am anxious to. Indeed, all of my brothers have come at my request because of the uncertainties I faced after Ma's death a few months ago. The whole family is coming together. That includes the two of you, as well."

"So the inn is becoming crowded." Faith stroked the cat's fur, its contented rumbling audible in the still afternoon air. "Don't ask us to leave without you, my dear. That option is not available."

"That's not how I want your help." Cassie glanced between the two women, aware to her core of the power flowing through their veins. "My family is expanding and I want you to work with the rest of us to remove the gang's threat to all of us."

"What gang?" Hope straightened in her seat.

"We think the group of men who have been meeting in the dining room are behind the killing of witches." Cassie pushed away the remembered terror of the most recent attack of her person. "Would you consider working with me and my brothers to expose them and bring them to justice? As long as they're threatening witches, none of us are safe."

"Including Cassie." Giles tapped his fist on the thick wood mantel. "She was attacked yesterday morning right here in this room."

"Have you apprehended the varmint?" Hope sprang to her feet, frowning at Giles. "That's your job, after all."

"He ran away." Giles shuttered his expression, the slip painful to his pride.

"The point is, a man rushed in with a knife with the intent of killing me because I'm a witch." Keeping her voice even took every ounce of her willpower. Presenting any weakness to her aunts might prove disastrous. "Giles stopped him and chased him off. But he's still out there. Threatening others. We can't let him continue."

"And may try again." Giles moved away from the fireplace to stand by Cassie's chair. "That's why I'm sticking close."

Cassie flashed a grateful smile at her brother before regarding her aunts in turn. "With your help, we can expose the gang and bring them to justice. To end this awful witch hunt once and for all. Only then can we be safe when we use our magic to help others."

Faith grimaced, stroking the black fur with precise motions. "Why for the love of all that is witchcraft would you want to use your abilities to help others?"

"It's the right thing to do. Helping others." What a question. Revealing as to her aunts' view of their own talents and powers. "Will you help us?"

Hope spun around, her long black skirts flaring and swirling about her black shoes. "I'll wipe them all off the face of the earth and then nobody will be bothered by their pathetic presence."

"Wipe them...kill them?" A shudder racked Cassie's shoulders as she blinked at her aunts with growing horror in her chest. "That's not what I asked."

"They have the audacity to attack witches, to threaten our niece." Hope flicked her hand, her long fingers a waterfall of contempt. "'Twould be best if they no longer existed."

Faith paused in her obsessive stroking to pin Cassie with a sneer. "Just say the word, my dear, and we'll take care of the matter."

Cassie swallowed hard. The very concept of her aunts taking such drastic measures on her behalf made her ill. Killing must be a last resort. Hope and Faith contemplated lowering themselves to the same level as the men who killed their sister, as the men who killed other women suspected of being witches. Instead of holding themselves to a higher standard. Killing couldn't be the only way when people disagreed with each other.

"No, that's not the answer." She stood and paced to the fireplace to stare at the flickering flames for a few seconds. Then she turned to face her aunts. "I can't condone your approach to solving the matter. It's wrong to kill unless absolutely necessary for your survival."

"Well, isn't it true they want to kill you?" Hope folded her arms over her slender chest. "They tried once. What's to stop them from succeeding next time?"

"Me." Giles strode forward to glare at Hope. "The sheriff and deputy are aware of the situation. If we can provide even a shred of evidence, they'll arrest the men. None of us need to resort to lethal means to defend against them. If we can determine who they follow, we can stop them all by stopping that man. Without killing anyone."

"Our way is faster and cleaner." Faith rubbed her cat's ears to louder purring. "No one could trace anything to us. Let us take care of it."

Cassie shook her head, her blond curls dancing across her shoulders. "No, thank you." Bitter at the turn of the conversation, Cassie glared at her aunts. "But if you change your mind, we're having a family meeting in here after the supper rush."

How dare they even think she'd consider going after a dozen men with the intent of killing them all? To her mind such a plan had no business being considered for even a moment. Better to leave it up to the lawmen to take those who were guilty of hunting witches into custody to face a judge.

"Giles, I need to go to work. Are you coming?" She worried her bottom lip as she contemplated the hard expressions on the other women's faces. Then she met his gaze.

"Right behind you." Giles glanced at Hope and Faith. "I hope you'll think about what Cassie proposed. You're family and as my mother is fond of saying, we're stronger together."

"Or weaker if you're going down the path of being a do-gooder." Hope motioned to her sister. "I'm going back up. Are you coming?"

Faith gathered Malachi in her arms and stood. "I knew this conversation would be a waste of time."

Cassie stared at her and then at Hope, thinking how different they were from even her mother's cynical view of the world. How could she possibly sway them her way? As she considered various arguments, she discarded them as quickly. Her aunts had been brought up under her grandfather's strident and stringent dictates toward protecting what he counted as his property, his rights, his goals. Yet she heard the man died striving but failing to protect those very things. Would her aunts follow in those footsteps as well? What could Cassie possibly say to them to convince them to try her approach?

"I wish you'd think about what I ask. Our family is more important and more powerful when we unite. Or could be."

Hope leveled a disbelieving glare at her. "Go play your songs and sing your ditties, child."

"Fine." Cassie clutched her skirts in both hands to keep her from futilely lashing out with frustration and anger. "Let's go, Giles. I have ditties to sing."

She marched out of the room, not looking back. What had possessed her to put herself in such a vulnerable position with respect to how her aunts would regard her? Somehow, someway, she needed to find a way to convince them around to her way of thinking. But how?

Despite the large group gathering around the family's dining room table, Silas couldn't stop the niggling doubts rankling inside. His senses thrummed with warning about a building climax of danger. Giles closed the doors and then strode to the head of the table, standing with hands pressed to the wood. Slowly the chatter died out as the others waited for his guidance.

Silas characterized each person's expression as silence fell. Flint, stony faced, sat beside Cassie, who struggled silently to keep an open mind. Silas sensed her mounting inner conflict and wondered at the cause. Allegro perched on the back of a chair, his wings folded neatly at his sides as his intelligent gaze roamed the room. Silas realized he could no longer sense his sister's feelings, since she'd raised her protective barrier. Did she not want him to know how conflicted she was or was something else at play? Beside Cassie, Abram subtly fidgeted with the points of his vest, betraying his own agitation. Daniel occupied a chair at the foot of the table, clenched jaw and tapping forefinger revealing his feelings on the family meeting. Meg and Myrtle sat opposite Cassie and beside Silas, seemingly relaxed and yet poised and ready. Who was missing?

Silas racked his brain. Mercy. Hope. Faith. The three sisters who had in one sense started all of the turmoil in the family by keeping secrets and fighting among themselves. Cassie longed for their father to return to deal with them, but could he? Did he truly have the means with which to calm the long-standing anger and distrust between them?

"It's time for two things." Giles scanned the group around the large table. "First, we welcome two new members to our family. Myrtle and Megara Marple have just come into their special abilities as elves. Welcome, ladies."

Myrtle nodded as the others lightly clapped their welcome. "Thank you. We will assist any way we can."

"If you'll forgive my inquisitiveness," Abram interjected, "might you explain what your special abilities are?"

"We'll get to that in a moment." Giles waved off the question. "Be patient."

Giles' own impatience simmered inside of him. Silas followed Cassie's lead and raised his defenses to protect himself from the swirling emotions around him. Having gleaned the temperature of the room, he elected to home in on what Giles had to say next.

"Then move along, brother, as we're all on tenterhooks waiting for the other shoe to fall." Daniel drummed his fingers on the table for a moment and then made a fist. "Why are we here?"

"To catalog our powers and abilities so we know how we can work together against the various threats aimed at us." Giles perused the group with a slight frown on his brows. "I suppose I'll start."

A shimmering in the air drew Silas' attention to the end of the table. Behind Daniel, Mercy came into view. "What's this?"

Daniel jumped in his seat and twisted around to glare at his mother. "Again?" He huffed his aggravation into the early evening quiet. "Why don't you take a seat over there, Ma?"

Mercy chuckled as she glided around the table to take an empty chair beside Silas. "Proceed, Giles."

Sarcasm dripped from Giles' voice as he continued. "Thank you, mother. Like I was saying, as the family Guardian, I am empowered with superhuman strength along with the ability to silently communicate with Cassie. As such, she can warn me of when she's in danger and then I can evaluate what assistance to provide. Flint, why don't you go next and we'll go around the table from there?"

"Fine." Flint shrugged a shoulder as he peered around

the table. "I have my wits and the pistol Silas gave me with which to defend any of you. And I can communicate with ghosts, should that prove necessary. Cassie?"

Flint's list of skills didn't impress but the courage and strength he brought to the table did. Without a doubt, he'd move mountains to protect Cassie. To serve and defend those under his care. His sister found a very worthy mate.

"My voice and the effects I can create with it continue to strengthen. Coupled with my songspells I'm working on so I can influence others and my ability to communicate with both Silas and Giles through our thoughts and feelings, I've so far been able to stay safe. Those are the main things. I think that's it, but Ma tells me my powers grow with each family member who arrives. So what will I be able to do once Pa is home? And brings an aunt and uncle with him? So we'll see. Abram, your turn."

Abram cleared his throat. "I can shift into any other living being, including Cassie. I've practiced that before to attempt to protect her even if it did complicate things. I've also successfully become a cat, a bear, and a porcupine, too. Daniel?"

"It's about *time*." Daniel guffawed at his own lame joke. "Get it?"

"Just get on with it, will you?" Giles shook his head at his younger brother. "Tell us about time."

"Well, you know I can move from place to place in our current time. I did so when I took Abram and Cassie to our aunts' home and back again. I can also move between times, to the past or the future. I went back in time, for instance, to try to save our cousin from drowning, although I failed. I did learn that it's better to not try to change the past but to learn from it. Having the ability to transport two others from one place to another could be very useful indeed." He angled his head as he gazed at the younger of the Marple sisters. "Meg? I'm very curious to know what you can now do, other than work in the kitchen of course."

"I bet you are." Meg folded her hands in her lap. "I can control the flow of liquids with a thought. Given how close we are to the river and the falls above, that could be useful indeed. Just how these abilities can work together is an entirely different matter."

"I'm sure Giles is working that out in his mind as we share, sister." Myrtle flashed a grin at Giles, standing straight at the head of the table. "My gift complements Megara's. I can move objects with a thought. So I could create or remove any hazards or barriers as needed. Or get a cup of coffee if so desired." She chuckled as she glanced to Silas. "What's your gift?"

Silas hesitated, trying to sum up his special ability in a few words. "I can communicate silently with others, and sense their emotions. And I can craft powerful spells. Although I'm not sure how useful that might be if we're in some kind of fight."

Giles lifted a shoulder in a lazy shrug. "We'll see. Ma, tell us your abilities."

Mercy folded her translucent arms in front of her light blue dress as she relaxed in the chair. "I've learned that I can communicate with other haints in the area."

"You can become corporeal for a time as well," Cassie added. "I've seen you knock down Aunt Hope."

Mercy slowly shook her head. "It's becoming more difficult, but yes, I still can do that."

Giles tapped his fingers on the table to draw everyone's attention. "The variety of abilities we bring to this group should yield quite a defense. But with our father returning soon with his more powerful warlock talents we should be even stronger."

"Uncle Beck and Aunt Scarlet also bring gifts we're not aware of yet." Abram shifted in his seat, draping his wrists over the ends of the armrests of his chair. "With the number of tools in our toolbox, we should be well prepared to defend ourselves and protect Cassie from harm."

"You're right, Abram. Only..." Allegro flapped his wings as Cassie glanced sharply at Abram. "I mean, I agree that it's quite an array but is it enough? Are *we* enough?"

Silas focused on his sister for a long moment, not surprised that her protective barrier slipped for a flash of time revealing her worry. Sure, she tried to hide it behind her brave talk, but inside she remained concerned and defensive. All he could do was to stay close and be acutely aware of every nuance of her emotional state. Only then could he, and they by extension, provide the best security possible for her welfare. But as she said, would it be enough?

So where are they? I've called an urgent meeting with my men after the dismal results of the last attempt to handle the witch. To remove her from the center of the maelstrom of evil surrounding the ill-fated inn. The men gathered at the table in the dining room have come at my summons. We must overcome the growing threat to our community. The young blond witch is being watched, guarded. Otherwise Larry would have succeeded in his mission of killing her. But where were all the Fairhopes? And Flint? They normally hunkered in the dining room of an evening, flaunting their coven of crones. Only the two older crones sat at their usual table, whispering and plotting who knows what devilish tricks.

I need to know what the others think. Perhaps they've seen or heard something useful to direct our next steps in our aim to rid the region of these witches. "So, gentlemen, I appreciate your turning out at such a late hour. I've heard that Mr. Reginald Fairhope is on his way home and bringing more mischief with him in the form of a brother and sister. If they are anything like him, then they are involved in magic as well. The family will grow stronger as a result. We must stop that from happening."

A shift at the front of the room made me look at the two older women. They'd first shown up months ago and seemed to inflict their presence on the family. To what end? The older one stared at me, her eyes piercing my soul. I blinked and looked away, denying her access to my deepest thoughts and concerns. The other with her black cat on the seat beside her, stared at me, lips flat, brows furrowed. What were they up to? Nothing good, not from the look of them. I'll take care of them next. Turning my attention back to my men, I dismissed the old women from my thoughts.

"How do you propose to stop them?" One of the men sporting a long gray beard asked in a steady voice. "The two attempts to take out Miss Fairhope failed."

"I'm well aware. She's being guarded which tells us how important she is to the family. Without her, they will have to regroup which will delay any plans they are making. We mustn't fail the next time."

Larry grimaced. "I'm sorry. Giles startled me by returning so quickly."

"Somehow he was alerted to your attack." But how? I've

sneaked into the room where Larry went after the witch. The man couldn't see through the sturdy walls. I don't think so, anyway. "Do you have any idea how he knew you were there?"

Larry shook his head. "He just came barging into the room. I fled rather than being caught and beaten."

"Wise move all things considered." The oldest boy was stronger than an ox and more dangerous than a charging bull. I surveyed the men gazing expectantly at me. The new man, young and ambitious, had some unique skills with a knife and a garrote. Perhaps he'd have better luck. "You. I want you to handle this situation, quickly and quietly."

Gray eyes regarded him steadily and then blinked once. "Thank you, sir."

The pale gray color reminds me of my mother's loving eyes. She'd been stalwart during chaotic times of my childhood and young adult years. She'd been there to comfort when I fell ill with a fever. She'd guided me through my awkward attempts at courting young women, eventually helping me to win the hand of my beloved wife. Chided me into being the best man I could be, teaching me how to be a gentleman in every sense of the title. Educated, well read, polite, and an upstanding citizen. Then she was taken from me by the curse an old wrinkled, angry witch had pronounced on her head. A curse my mistakes had brought down upon her. A curse that sucked the joy, the hope, the very life from my mother's body. As dirt covered my mother's coffin, I vowed revenge against witches.

"Do not fail me." As I looked around at the somber faces, one stood out as hesitant. Wary. Resistant to my goals. I'll have to keep an eye on him. He may be growing a conscience. "I will not tolerate another failure. Understood?"

Chapter Fourteen

How about this?" Cassie struck a few chords on the piano, glad the breakfast rush had ended, leaving behind only a few straggling guests to witness her attempts at a protection spellsong. She'd play softly and keep her voice low, unobtrusively so, while they sorted out the lyrics. With good fortune, they'd continue to ignore her attempts at crafting a protection spellsong. "Is it forceful enough?"

"I think so, but the lyrics..." Silas studied the paper before him, stanzas of words written, crossed out, and rewritten.

Her brother amazed her with his way with words. She'd known, of course, that he made his living writing articles about the places and people he encountered. Watching him draft the words to the protection spellsong gave her even more reason to be proud of him. He chose each word with extreme care and a deep awareness of nuance behind the meanings. He had a gift for selecting the perfect word. Even if he didn't think so.

Mandy strolled across the floor, pushing a chair in at one table, repositioning a vase of flowers at another. She stopped to inspect the other tables with a critical gaze before walking over to the bar where Flint worked on organizing the colorful bottles of liquor. Preparing for the lunch rush in a couple of hours when more working men would stop in for a hot meal and a refreshing ale. Hope and Faith with her blasted cat sat at their usual table not far from the piano, their presence a constant annoying warning. Larry hurried over to her aunts' table to dole out mugs of cider with a flourish. Apparently they planned to stay awhile. Lovely. Better to focus on the task at hand, that of creating a much-needed protection spellsong.

Silas tapped a dull pencil against his cheek as he scowled at the words scrawled on the paper in front of him. Crumpling the page, he shook his head. "The tune works but these lyrics are flat and useless. I'll try again."

His frustration assailed her core. "They weren't that bad. Don't throw them away."

"They need to be the right words in the right order to do their job most effectively. They need to not only rhyme to some degree but also contain the necessary intent, your will, as you sing them." He squeezed the wad of paper into a smaller ball, but didn't release his grip. "It's my way of helping to protect you, by crafting the strongest spell possible."

She played around with the tune some more, quietly humming along as she considered his deep-seated concerns. His fear of letting her down in her time of need. Of demonstrating to his brothers that he wasn't as good as them. That his words didn't hold a flicker of light to their brighter candles of magical abilities. Of proving his parents right in sending him away to face the world on his own. Self-doubt threatened to consume him. She struck a harsh chord to draw his attention.

"What was that for?" Tossing the ball between his hands, Silas stared at her.

You know very well. Your special way with words is a very powerful gift. I believe you can write a spell into that song that will protect not only me but others when I need to do so.

I'm trying—

You have to believe in yourself. She shook her head slowly at him as she played softly, switching to her calming spellsong.

This spell has to be very powerful. I've just started learning how to craft a spell let alone one to protect anyone. Ma made it very clear in our practice session the other day about how important word choice is, along with the rhythm and repetition of them, to support and strengthen the power behind the spell.

It's daunting, I know. But I also know you can do it.

How can you possibly know that?

She lifted her hands from the keys and raised her chin. "Because I know you. You can do this, Silas. For all of us, but mostly for yourself."

"I'll try."

She indicated the ball of paper with a tilt of her head. "Smooth that out and I think you'll see it's not as bad as you thought. Oh, hi, Giles." She smiled at her brother as he strolled up to the piano, guitar in hand.

Her gaze snagged on the dark look the waiter aimed her direction. Larry's frown lingered for two beats before vanishing when Mandy brushed past him. He said something that made her laugh as she went to greet two men at the door. Then he shot Cassie another solemn look, dark purpose behind it swamping her senses. She blinked at the sudden shift but he'd turned away when she looked again. Had she imagined his contempt?

"Can I join you two?" Giles hefted the instrument with a questioning lift of a brow. "I heard you playing and thought it might be fun."

"Pull up a chair." Cassie contemplated sharing her concern about Larry with the Guardian but hesitated, uncertain of whether she'd correctly interpreted his look. Giles would protect her from anyone, including Larry, so she decided to ignore the fleeting concern. She glanced at Silas. *Ready to try this again?*

He shrugged as he finished spreading the wrinkled page out on the cloth-covered table. Peering at Giles he motioned to the page. "Let me make a tweak or two while you warm up."

Giles contemplated the condition of the sheet of paper before regarding Cassie. "Play that tune again and I'll pick up when I can."

She started playing, keeping the tempo at a moderate pace so Giles could become acquainted with the new tune. He listened for several measures and then joined in, strumming and correcting his chords to adjust to the variations in the music. She kept aware of Silas' emotions as he erased and scribbled on the lyrics. With each change he grew more confident in the subtle differences to the spell woven into the song. Keeping the words meaningful and thus effective as a protective force without overtly revealing the true nature was difficult. She couldn't know what changes he'd made until he shared them with her, but she could tell they bolstered his surety of their power.

A wave of confusion swept through her, forcing her eyes

to survey the few guests now watching the trio around the piano. Without knowing what they were listening to, they seemed to be wary of the music. She eased a gentle smile on her lips as she nodded reassurance to the audience. The combination of guitar and piano evoked a stronger reaction than they'd otherwise have experienced. Yet again. She rested her gaze on Giles as he focused on matching his chords to the tune. His strength carried over to his music which supported her playing and ultimately her singing. All of which increased the influence of her voice over those listening. Even if they didn't know what exactly they were listening to.

"Klee! Klee!"

She looked sideways just in time to see Allegro flash through the open window at the back of the dining room. He darted around the room, flew close to drop a pinecone on the polished surface of the piano, and then alighted on the rack beside the square piano. Her familiar liked to bring her small gifts when he returned from his surveillance flights. Simply letting her know all was well by bringing something innocuous. Like the perfectly formed pinecone.

A reminder to gather the decorations for the Allhallows Eve gathering in only eight days. She had time to dye the cones various colors, add a bit of ribbon to them and hang them around the dining room. Her pumpkins, destined to be carved into fun or scary faces, were ready to harvest as well. She'd already gathered the apples, sitting in baskets in the cold cellar to keep fresh. Next week she'd send Teddy out to gather some wildflowers and ferns in the woods and along the river. She planned to use them so the guests could make wreaths for doors and rings for tables, depending on the quantity he collected.

"What did he bring you?" The deep voice raised her gaze from the pinecone to smile up at Flint as he stopped by the piano.

"A harbinger of autumn." She finished the song and rested her hands in her lap. "Another reminder of a long list of chores to accomplish before the party."

"Only days away, I know." Flint nodded a greeting to Giles and then Silas. "The music sounds good and the audience seems to like it."

Silas grimaced at him. "I just need to finish the lyrics and then they can try it all together."

"Pulling the pieces together would help, I'm sure." Flint examined the pinecone then glanced up. "There's Matt. I wonder what he needs."

The man in question hurried toward them, his dark eyes serious and his strides purposeful. He halted beside Flint with a nod to Cassie before addressing his boss. "I've been thinking..."

Flint waved him into silence. "I was about to seek you out. What can I do for you?"

"First, thank you for the additional kitchen help. That's made my job much easier."

"The customers like the results as well. Go on."

"The Marple sisters are even faster than before...before they became elves, I mean." He slowly shook his head. "This place sure attracts a variety of people. About the party menu..."

"I thought we'd settled that?" Flint canted his head, his confusion flowing into the air around him.

Cassie felt his concern mingling with the confusion. He'd already begun making final preparations for both the open house and the senator's visit. With her father and his critical eye days away from coming home, her beau wanted everything to be ready for both major events. As did she. His agitation increased, making Cassie raise her inner barrier and start playing her calming spellsong.

"I had an idea of how we can step up the desserts but it would require sending for some ingredients posthaste." Matt folded his arms as he scanned the faces watching him. "Nothing too expensive but they'd be a welcome addition I believe."

"We can discuss it in the kitchen rather than here in front of our guests." Flint shifted his weight to stand evenly balanced. "I'd rather not get their hopes up just in case."

Cassie quietly played the piano, Giles softly strumming an accompanying harmony. A sense of peace and contentment pervaded the dining room. Even Flint relaxed and seemed more at ease in his own skin. She perused the others in the room, delighted to find everyone calm and content. Then she met John Baker's steady gaze and a frisson of worry shivered down her spine. Something in his gaze, in the steady flow of anxiety emanating from deep inside him, set off internal alarms. Allegro hopped sideways, flapping his wings in reaction to her sudden agitation. Giles and Silas both glanced sharply at her, questions flickering in their eyes. She shook her head once, not willing to put her feelings into words. But of course, with these two brothers words were unnecessary to convey those feelings.

"Silas, let's try your new lyrics, shall we?" She held out her hand, waiting for him to slowly nod as a dawning understanding made him place the paper in her fingers. "Let's see." She perused the words, nodding to herself as she pressed her lips together. "This is perfect. Giles, you ready to try the song?"

"I'll follow your lead." Giles cradled the guitar, ready to play when she began.

She carefully propped the page on the piano and pressed the ivories to start playing the introduction to the tune. Then she sang the spellsong, checking for any impacts the spell had on those in the room. Especially John Baker.

I shall prevail not quake nor fear
Right and might remain at my side
Truth resides here
While charms still abide
To fight my foes. Right will not hide.

When she'd finished, she stood to accept the smattering of applause in the room. As her gaze landed on John, he slowly nodded at her. He was no longer anxious. On the contrary. He was determined.

Traffic approaching the inn increased as the sun neared its zenith the next morning. Silas relaxed on the front porch, legs stretched before him, hands folded over his abdomen. Peace and quiet rattled around inside despite the hubbub of horse-drawn carriages, oxen-pulled wagons, and dogs nosing about. While some would find it enjoyable to have the time to stare at the comings and goings without needing to join in, echoes of his travels haunted his memories. He came to the inn last of his brothers, arrived to find them settling in for the duration and then some. Giles had hinted that Silas consider doing the same thing, but could he? Did he have the ability to settle in one place? He'd been on the trails and roads for years. He'd been one of the men riding up to the hitching rail to dismount wearily but feeling accomplished, ready for a hot meal and a cold brew.

"Comfortable?" Daniel halted beside the empty chair across the table from Silas. "Want some company?"

"Have a seat." Silas pushed to an upright position, drawing his feet to rest flatfooted on the wooden porch floor. He gestured to the sawdust on Daniel's sleeve. "What have you been doing?"

Glancing to his arm, Daniel smirked and brushed away the dust. "Sanding the wood around a doorframe to ready it for painting." He angled the chair to face Silas more and dropped into it. "I need a respite, that's all."

"I hear you've agreed to instruct young Teddy." Another indicator that his brothers intended to become fixtures in the region.

"I have indeed." Daniel nodded slowly as he surveyed their surroundings. "I intend to explore further whether it would be viable to open a school, or simply offer my services as a tutor."

"Becoming a lettered gentleman would benefit many young men, I am certain." Where would he be without his own literary education? He'd not be penning articles. "Cassie seems to think Teddy has some talent with regard to his intellect. I hope he won't be a waste of your time."

Daniel glanced sharply at him, a slight frown hovering over his brow. "I dare say he is adept and will be a joy to teach."

"Isn't that his father's job?" Silas studied the conflicting emotions flitting across his brother's face. "What?"

"Have you met his father? Do you know who he is?" Daniel's gaze sharpened the longer he stared at Silas. "He's one of the men responsible for our mother's death."

"Oh, him." Silas recalled the harsh features, the bedraggled attire, and the sense of despair and anger pervading the man's soul. "I see."

"I wouldn't send an intelligent, savvy, impressionable young man back into that world for anything." Daniel's gaze slid away from Silas to stare unseeing across the carriageway. "I'd sooner lock him up and throw away the key. The end result would be the same."

"But—"

"Damnation. Here he comes." Daniel pushed to his feet, crossing his arms over his heaving chest. "He can't have him back."

"Who?" Silas also stood to gaze down the lane to where the man in question stalked toward them. He reached out to him, sensed yet again the anger but also hope. For what did he hope though? "I wonder what he wants."

"My money is on his son." Daniel braced his feet apart as if preparing for battle. "I hope Teddy stays away during this conversation."

"It would be best for him to not be present." But someone else should be. *Cassie. Come to the porch. Teddy's dad is coming.*

Oh, dear. On my way.

"We'll take him out of sight and deal with him. Cassie is also coming out to confront the man." Silas tapped the table with his fingertips to dispel the growing sense of agitation in his core.

"Oh, good. I'm glad she'll be here as well." Daniel bobbed his head several times and then stared at the scowling face of Adam Jacobs. "I hope she hurries."

"I'm here." Cassie closed the front door behind her before she marched across the porch to wait at the top of the steps. "He's very angry. This won't be easy."

Adam halted at the bottom of the steps for a moment, and then stomped up to stand in front of Cassie. "Where's my son?"

"Doing his studies, Mr. Jacobs." Cassie clasped her hands before her and held her ground. "He's safe and healthy and doing well."

"Send for him. I'm takin' him home." Adam's scowl hardened into a glare. "He's mine."

Daniel strode to confront the bristling man. Silas watched the silent exchange between the two men, each declaring in stance and expression their attitude toward the other. Silas reached out to both, sensed his brother's adamant defense of the boy's right to a better life and then sensed the grief and desperation of the boy's father. Cassie kept her unwavering gaze on Adam, her determination to protect the boy from the evil ways of his father uppermost in her heart.

Silas stepped forward to do what he could to avert an argument that would draw unwanted attention from the passing guests. As it was, they cast suspicious and cautious glances at the tense group gathered at the top of the porch steps. Flint would have their hides if they caused a scene that would reflect unfavorably upon the establishment and its owners.

"Come with me where we can speak more privately on this matter." Silas urged the others to walk with him, reaching out to encourage with his empathic ability as he used his arms to herd them down the porch. Once he had them around the side of the inn, he stopped and gathered them into a small circle in the shade of the building. "This is better. Mr. Jacobs, I can sympathize with you as far as not having your son's company or assistance. However..."

"I need him home to help." Adam glanced around the group, his eyes narrowing. "He's got chores to do at home more urgent than y'all need here. You've got plenty of others to help. I've just got my son."

"But now it's just you at your house. You want what's best for your son, don't you?" Silas regarded the man, delving into his emotional state to refine his arguments. "In your own way, you love the boy. You've seen how smart he is. You've even thought he'd make something of himself when he grows up."

Adam shifted his gaze to peer at Silas with suspicion. "You trying to twist a man's love of his son into something bad?"

"Oh, no sir!" Silas waved off the suggestion. "I merely mean that you're smart enough to recognize the potential in your son."

Cassie softly started humming, then added words to the quiet tune. Her protection spellsong. He trained his gaze on Adam instead of allowing himself even a glimpse at her face. *What are you doing?*

Just keep talking while I keep singing.

Ah. I see. "Mr. Jacobs. Please listen to me when I say that we all have Teddy's safety and well-being as a priority. We can also see what you see. The boy has a wealth of potential to grow into a fine man with a fine education. Daniel, here, is a college instructor and will be his tutor to ensure he receives the best learning possible."

Adam flicked a glance at Cassie, his frown dipping and then lifting as he studied her. He turned back to Silas. "You'll teach him? Make him an upstanding citizen instead of following in my beggarly ways? I don't want him being no thief or murderer when I knows he could be so much more. Can you give him that?"

Cassie continued her singing, increasing the volume a little at a time. She nodded at Adam, smiling softly as the song flowed from her lips.

"That's a question for Daniel." Silas arched a brow at his brother. "Can you give him that?"

"Indeed I can and I intend to." Daniel stuck out his hand to Adam. "I give you my word."

Adam assessed the expressions on each of the men's faces and then accepted Daniel's handshake. "Fine. I think you're right it's in Teddy's interest to stay with you. I guess I should thank you for giving him this opportunity, for taking care of him and showing him how to be better than I can teach him. I'll take my leave then. Tell the boy I love him and hope he turns out fine."

Silas offered his hand to the man. "I'll be sure to relay your message."

Adam shook his hand and then met Cassie's gaze as she fell silent. "I know you've taken him under your wing despite what I've done. Thank you for believing in him enough to fight for him when his old man didn't."

"My pleasure, Mr. Jacobs. You take care and we'll take care of him. I promise." Cassie folded her hands at her waist. "If it's all right with you, I'll let him know he can always visit you."

"That would be fine. Thank you." Adam nodded once and then spun on his heel and started walking away, shaking his head slowly as he went.

Silas watched his ambling gait for a moment and then grinned at Cassie. "You did that. Used your protection songspell coupled with my words, my suggestions, to convince him to let Teddy stay."

"Who, me?" She batted her eyelashes at him and then chuckled. "Looks like we make quite a team."

Chapter Fifteen

After Adam left, Silas moseyed into the kitchen to grab a snack and escaped out back to the porch. Alone. His brothers bonded together when faced with challenges while he required his own space in which to think and process. He'd stumbled upon so much he didn't know about his family. Most of what he'd learned he could fit into a picture, much like a nearly completed jigsaw puzzle. Only, a few pieces seemed to be missing. One thing for certain. He'd discover where those pieces hid.

The confrontation with the boy's pa ended far easier than anyone could have anticipated. Cassie's quick thinking and sweet, potent voice made the difference. Blending together their unique powers created a fine magical dish. Knowing the variety of available abilities they possessed among all of the creatures at the inn raised interesting possibilities.

Footfalls on the porch boards behind him made him swivel his head to see who approached. His surprise must have shown on his face as she halted. "Aunt Faith, how nice to see you on this fine afternoon."

She hesitated, her long, sable skirts swishing about her shoes, her familiar black and white cat pacing beside her. She raised her chin and observed him. "I needed some air while my sister naps."

While Faith knew where Hope would be for a while, in other words. Silas refrained from sharing his interpretation of her comment. Perhaps he'd take the opportunity to see what missing pieces he could find by conversing with his aunt. Find out more about her motivation for lingering at the inn although not wanted. "Please, join me. It's a fine day for gazing at the leaves on the trees and the clouds drifting by."

Faith glided to the opposite chair and settled gracefully onto the seat. "It is indeed a lovely day. What brings you out here all alone?"

He shrugged, buying time to marshal his thoughts. "I have a few things I wished to ponder without distractions. Oh, no—" He waved her back in her seat. "I've had my ponder and welcome your company. Don't go on my account."

Two could bluff at this game of deception swaddled in polite discourse. What brought her out without her sister to seek him? Her curiosity warred with concern. About what?

"I don't wish to intrude, but if you're quite sure." She relaxed into her seat, letting her gaze drift across the foothills bedecked in orange, gold, and maroon, with dark evergreens stitching the other colors together. "I do envy this view. We don't see anything so beautiful from our house."

"That's one reason I enjoy my travels, having the variety of experiences that moving from one place to another provides." He followed her gaze, seeing the sight as if for the first time and appreciating it all over again. "I think each place has its charms."

"Magical or otherwise, I assume you mean?" She chuckled lightly, her familiar glancing up at her as she did so.

Silas peered at his aunt, realizing it was the first time she'd laughed in his presence. "Indeed. Is Aunt Hope feeling well? I hope she's not having a headache."

"She's merely tired after working on a new potion last night during the cusp of the full moon. She'll be right as rain when she rises."

"I am impressed by witches who can brew potions as well as create the necessary medicines we rely upon." Silas studied the foothills rather than look at his aunt. He didn't want to set off any alarms before he had the chance to ask a pointed question and assess her reaction. He'd contemplated Hope's claim that Faith was out in search of herbs the day George died. Her activities that fateful day remained obscured. "If only she'd had some kind of potion or simple to save her son's life when my pa brought his body home. Life would have been different for all of us."

"I don't see how." The weight of Faith's gaze lasted for three beats of his heart. Malachi jumped into her lap while her quizzical expression turned stony. "What are you implying?"

Concern flared in his aunt's chest, which she quickly squashed beneath a veneer of disregard. As if she could sense his probing of her emotions. Interesting. And enlightening. She adjusted her projected emotions to suit her aims. What if he asked a more direct question?

"Aunt Faith, your sister told me you weren't at home when my pa brought George's body home. Where were you? I know Aunt Hope could have used your support."

His aunt automatically stroked the cat's soft fur. "I was taking care of an errand. Hope didn't seriously need my help. She's strong and able to manage on her own."

A stroke of distrust flashed like lightning through Silas. His aunt was a moment too late in shielding her emotions, allowing him to detect her mistrust of her sister. Something related to their...father. From what Silas had read about his grandfather, he was the one who couldn't be trusted. He had his own agenda and questionable aims. Whatever it was that Faith hid from him, and from his aunt, it had something to do with his grandfather. That couldn't be good.

He'd go back to the attic and delve more deeply into the papers—letters, flyers, newspapers, and more—his mother had saved. Hiding among them lurked the missing pieces to the puzzle of his family's past.

Some days it would have been best to stay abed. Flint stood by the front door of the General Store on the Square in Huntsville, impatiently waiting for Cassie and Mandy to finish making their selections. A process which dragged on interminably. He had better things to be doing but he couldn't argue with the need to purchase the necessary food stuffs to augment Matt's new and improved menu for the gathering. Nor with the need to pick out whatever they deemed necessary for decorations and the crafts they planned for the younger guests. Did it have to take hours, though?

"Stop tapping your foot." Giles huffed a laugh from where he'd taken up a defensive position beside him. "You act like a school boy instead of a gentleman."

"My feet wish to depart posthaste." Flint scanned the bustling store, seeking any unwarranted attention paid to either of the girls, but especially Cassie. Having her in town, in the too-crowded store, made him uneasy. For goodness sake, she wasn't safe in her own parlor. But she insisted she and Mandy would know what was right and proper so Flint had required Giles attend them as well. With two of them on guard, the girls should be safe. "I wish to take her to the haven of our home."

"Soon. They are nearly done. See?" Giles pointed to Mandy gathering up an assortment of small jars of paint and fine brushes while Cassie talked with the woman measuring lengths of ribbon and yards of cloth. "Calm down. We'll be on our way back soon."

The bell over the door jangled yet again. Flint turned to see who entered as Giles moved forward. Holding the door open, he greeted his fiancé. Haley Baker paused to smile up at him and then swished past him into the store. He let the door close with a bump as he rejoined Flint.

"I haven't see her in days. Yet it feels like weeks." Giles watched Haley make her way to the back of the store where Cassie waited for the sales woman to measure and cut lengths of variously colored ribbon.

"By the intense expression on their faces, it would seem the girls feel the same way." Haley angled her body toward Cassie as she spoke excitedly to her, gesturing with her hands and using a multitude of eyebrow moves. The range of emotions flitting across Cassie's face suggested her varying response to her friend's animation. Curiosity. Interest. Wariness. Hope. Acceptance. But of what? "I wonder what they're planning over there."

"Probably something feminine and thus of no interest to

us." Giles shook his head, chuckling. "Women. As long as they don't dabble in deceit, they can be quite lovely."

Although Flint possessed no empathic abilities like his beloved, still he could read the apparent reaction to the conversation across the room. He might not be magical but his human instincts had never failed him. Mandy joined the discourse with a growing excitement in her features. What were they plotting now?

As if on cue, Cassie turned to look at him, to meet his questioning gaze with a mysterious smile. Then she pointed to him and the other girls laughed, started gliding toward him, their long skirts brushing against each other with each stride. All three wore conspiratorial smiles.

"We'll soon find out. Here they come." Flint tilted his head in their direction. "Brace yourself."

"Oh, Giles, darling." Haley slipped her hand around Giles' elbow, sidling close to him. "I'm so glad you're here. It's such a nice surprise especially since I have a huge favor to ask."

Flint saw the big man stiffen at Haley's playful tone. He glanced at Cassie, noted the smug expression beneath the sparkle in her eyes. He tore his gaze away to focus on Giles' reluctant grin.

"And why is that?" Giles maintained a steady gaze despite the humor in his eyes.

"I've missed you so." Haley squeezed his arm, draping her other hand on top of the first. "And I need you to reassure Flint here that we'll be fine."

"What do you intend, my beloved?" Giles asked, slowly lifting one brow. "Nothing unsavory, I presume?"

"Of course not! I've simply invited Cassie and Mandy to Riverwood so we can speak in private about our wedding plans." She looked up at him from beneath her wide-brimmed bonnet. "I have the carriage waiting out front to drive us home."

"Wait a minute." Flint couldn't stop the interruption. "Are you proposing for the three of you ladies to travel alone to your home?"

"Indeed. How very quick of you." Haley shot him a sideways glance, sarcasm dripping from every word. "We'll be fine."

"No, I can't allow it." Flint's heart beat in his throat, making it difficult to breathe or speak. "It's not safe for any of you."

"But, Flint, you and Giles keep insisting there is safety in numbers." Cassie took hold of his hand, squeezing gently. "There will be three of us, two witches and one very capable young woman besides. What's the matter?"

Where to begin to define the problems with such a plan. They knew Cassie was being watched, someone waiting for their chance to attack yet again. They knew someone wanted all the witches in the region removed or killed, preferably the latter. He knew he couldn't survive without Cassie. If something should happen to her, his heart would shatter.

"I don't think it's a good idea." Flint stared into her eyes, saw the determination reflecting back at him. If she insisted, she'd defeat him with a smile, a wayward tear, even a flip of her hair. He didn't want to deny her anything. But... "Please don't."

She squeezed his hand again, her mirth sobering as she stared at him. She'd likely sensed the depth of his concern, indeed the fear, rattling around in his gut. He swallowed the lump in his throat, trying to force his heart to steady, calm.

She wouldn't risk her own life nor her future. He should trust her on that score. And yet... He couldn't lose her.

She firmed her lips. "I'm sure we can protect ourselves as long as we're together. We only intend to drive to Riverwood which isn't all that far. The road is busy so there will be even more security in the number of witnesses around. I really want to go, Flint, but only with your agreement."

"I'll take care of her." Haley smiled at Flint. "I promise. I won't let anything bad happen to her."

"What do you think, Giles?" Flint mentally crossed his fingers that the big man would back him up. Giles, the Guardian, who hovered over his little sister like a mother hen. Surely, he wouldn't agree to the three girls traveling alone.

He studied the three young ladies for a long moment before answering. "I trust Haley to use her abilities to protect herself and her friends. They won't actually be alone if there are three of them. And they do have some means of protecting themselves as long as they're alert and on guard." A slight frown pressed down his brows as he rested his eyes on Mandy, then Haley, and finally Cassie. Then he addressed Flint. "I think they'll be safe together."

"But—"

"I'm not going to be far behind them." Giles held up his hand to halt the rest of Flint's objection. "I understand your concern, my friend. I will follow them to ensure they arrive safe and sound at Riverwood. Will that satisfy your need to keep them all from harm?"

Was it possible for him to be overly protective? To overreact to the potential for danger? Perhaps his love for her clouded his common sense, confused his priorities. She deserved to have time with her friends. She was right to call him out on the idea that together they'd be safe. He'd said the same thing often enough. Was he wrong to want to keep her close? To try to protect her even against her own desires? He drew in a long, slow breath and released it on the count of five. Being a reasonable adult grew harder the more he fell in love with her. Yet he didn't want to break her spirit anymore than he would want to break the spirit of a young horse learning to be ridden for the first time. Her spitfire personality attracted him as much as her fair face and willowy body. He swallowed again, this time forcing the discomfort with his own attitude back under control.

"I apologize for my overreaction. I have always said there is safety with more people around." He moistened his lips, delaying for a moment. "I think you should have time with your friends, so go with my blessing."

"I promise to be careful." Cassie flung her arms around him and kissed him on the lips despite the public situation. "Thank you for understanding. We'll take all the necessary precautions."

"Trust me, Flint." Haley wrapped her arm around Cassie's waist, pulling her close, and then doing the same to Mandy. "They're in very good hands."

Flint regarded the eager smiles on the three girls' faces. Brushing aside his concern with difficulty, he nodded. Yet the worry lingered, the feeling he should object more strenuously. But at the same time, Haley was merely taking the girls to her home for an afternoon. Her mother would be there, even if John might be troublesome. They'd fairly ruled him out as the instigator, hadn't they? Actually going to his house was likely the safest place for Cassie. What could go wrong?

He kissed Cassie on the top of her head. "I hope you have a good time."

"I intend to. Thank you, Flint. Come on, girls, let's go before they change their minds." Cassie threw a last smile over her shoulder as she let Haley usher her and Mandy out of the General Store, the bell jangling wildly as they let the door slam behind them.

He stared at the closed door, looking through the window as they mounted the step into the open carriage and trundled away. A sudden sinking feeling weighed down his heart and raised his level of concern ever higher. He couldn't shake the accompanying feeling of danger. Or the thought that sprung unwanted into his mind. Would he ever see her again?

"So we're going to wear similar colors to our weddings?" Cassie asked, perusing the passing landscape from her seat beside Haley as the open carriage traveled the hard-packed Winchester Road. "I like that idea."

The trip from Huntsville back to Riverwood flew by. They'd barely had time to discuss their attire let alone touch on location or refreshments. As she'd predicted, they were not the only vehicles on the road. Wagons piled with hay. The mail coach lumbering by. Other ladies in their sporty carriages and gentlemen mounted on gleaming horses. Cassie sensed no troubles, no threats. It was refreshing.

"Not identical, of course." Haley sniffed as she shook her head, her hands steady on the reins. "It's not like we'll be competing with each other since we'll marry on different days. But I think they should be elegant and beautiful colors. Jewel tones, perhaps?"

"I prefer pastels." Mandy grunted softly as the carriage bounced over a shallow rut in the dirt road. "I'm glad the town has decided to have the men fix this road. It's about time."

"Rather inconvenient for our men to give up hours of time to work on smoothing it out." Haley steadied the horses around a bend. "Surely the city leaders could arrange for a road crew."

"As long as they keep it from washing out and causing overturns of carriages." Mandy gripped the edge of the seat. "We've had far too many accidents on this stretch."

"Smells like rain." Cassie lifted her nose, inhaling the tang signifying the advent of rain.

"I hope not. I hate driving in the rain." Haley slapped the traces on the horses' haunches. "Giddap there. I want to get home before the heavens open."

The carriage rounded the turn of the lane leading up to the manor house of Riverwood. Compared to the utilitarian construction of the Fury Falls Inn, the refined red brick and tan clapboard house with dark blue front door and shutters at the windows at the end of the carriageway invited visitors. Bushes and tall trees flanked the base of the sturdy structure while dark gray clouds built up behind the building, creating an eerie backdrop to the pretty home. Cassie hadn't visited the place before, only heard about it from her father and Haley. From them she understood it was one of the few plantation houses in the area as John had only fairly recently moved to the region, bringing his wealth with him. Unlike others, he didn't need to wait until agricultural efforts yielded the money to improve the land, build a fine home, and reap the benefits of both. Which also meant he didn't need to fit in with the rest of the farmers and up-and-coming plantation owners.

Cassie surveyed the property with her senses, seeking out the emotional status of those working and playing around and in the buildings. The normal combination of emotions flowed through her. Childish glee. Fatigue. Concern. Happiness. Contentment. The typical reactions people felt while doing day-to-day tasks. But where was John? She couldn't pinpoint his location nor his inner state. A lingering suspicion surrounded his activities even though they'd begun to suspect some other man orchestrated the killings. Still, better to not let her guard down around the man. She raised her inner barrier enough to protect herself but still enable her to be aware of any threats coming her way. Her nerves stood on edge the closer the carriage drew to the front steps.

Haley pulled on the traces to halt the pair of horses in front of the manor. "Come on and I'll show you around, Cassie." She looped the leather traces around the brake and then gathered her skirts to step down from the conveyance. "This is your first time, isn't it?"

"It is." Cassie dropped lightly to the ground, clutching her drawstring purse in one hand. She swept her gaze over the front of the large house, her mouth falling open. "You have a lovely home."

The front door swung open and John emerged to welcome them. "Come on in, ladies. Mrs. Baker has refreshments in the back parlor for you all."

Cassie stiffened as John loomed at the top of the steps. She reached out to sample his emotional state, finding wariness and a tinge of fear. An eagerness. Much like a man hunting a deer, stalking through the woods after his prey. Lurking behind trees, slipping through the underbrush until he could claim his prize. She wouldn't be his target. She raised her barrier higher, prepared to defend herself everyway she knew how. She simply didn't trust him.

"Tea sounds divine, Father." Haley motioned to Cassie and Mandy with a wave of a hand. "I'm parched, so let's hurry." She took hold of Mandy's hand and led the way up the steps and through the door.

John stood on the top step waiting for Cassie to climb the stone treads. A distant rumble hinted at the approach of a storm. She drew in a breath and mounted the steps to accompany her host inside. No matter how she felt, she needed to put on a brave front, act normally, to keep him from sensing any chinks in her emotional armor. "Thank you for your kindness, sir."

"It's my pleasure to welcome you to our home." John crooked his arm with a somber expression on his face. "Come with me."

As the front door closed behind her with a heavy thud, she paused to look around the large entrance hall. The tiled floor stretched away from her, a golden candelabra hung from the ceiling above her head, while a marble-topped, cherry table stood proudly at the center of the wall to her left. An enormous vase of flowers provided color against the pastoral scenes gracing the wallpaper. The mix of fall flowers lightened the worry in her chest if only for a moment.

"This is your first visit, is it not?" John inspected the space as if seeing it through her eyes. "Perhaps you'd enjoy a tour after some refreshments?"

"Haley wished to discuss wedding plans I believe." She suppressed a shiver. She'd rather not spend any more time with him than necessary. She didn't trust him despite what her senses told her. "Perhaps another time."

"Of course." He crooked his arm to accept her hand on his elbow. "Some tea and cakes then."

She let him lead her down the passageway to the back parlor but any hope for inner calm had shattered. Something was wrong. The sense of elation, of success, from the man beside her alarmed her without her being able to predict what might be the root of its existence. His relief at his success grew as they neared the doorway. She kept her fingers light on his arm with an extreme effort, not wishing to give him any hint of her inner turmoil and upset.

As they crossed the threshold of the small room, she took in the elegant surroundings. A large stone fireplace occupied the center of the far wall, red and yellow flames snapping around the pile of logs. The other ladies had arranged themselves on settees on either side of the fireplace. Between them a low cherry table displayed a shining silver coffee and tea service with a tiered stand presenting a variety of cakes and biscuits. A normal setting for afternoon tea and yet the feeling of discord and unease ricocheted through her. She must protect them from whatever avarice lurked in John's soul. She must separate herself from him so she could summon magic if necessary. She removed her hand from John's arm and crossed the floor to stop in front of the smiling group of ladies.

She nodded to Haley and Mandy and then addressed Mrs. Baker. "I'm pleased to see you're all safely ensconced for afternoon tea."

Mandy tilted her head slightly, indicating her awareness of the concern in Cassie's tone. "Won't you join us?"

"Yes, please, Cassie." Haley motioned to the empty seat beside Mandy. "We've been waiting for you."

Nothing in her friends' exchange suggested they felt uneasy about being in the parlor. Or about having John nearby. Maybe her imagination ran amok. Perhaps her instincts had overreacted after all. "Thank you." Cassie settled onto the empty seat beside Mandy, smoothing the gingham fabric of her dress over her knees.

"Cassandra, welcome to our home. Would you like tea?" Tabitha gracefully lifted the silver tea pot in anticipation of Cassie's response.

"Thank you." She smiled at Mrs. Baker. "One lump, please."

Tabitha used silver tongs to select a small lump of white sugar from a silver bowl on the tray. She slid it into the cup and then handed the cup and saucer to Cassie. "There you are, my dear. Now that you're finally here, all safe and sound, Mr. Baker has something he needs to tell you. Don't you, my dear?"

John cleared his throat as he took a position in front of the four women. A frown lowered his brows as he looked at each of them, his gaze finally resting on Cassie. "I insist you remain here."

Her hand froze halfway to bringing the cup to her lips. There was the threat. He wished to kidnap her. Probably to turn her over to the man behind the scenes running the witch hunt. She lowered the porcelain cup to the saucer and then held on to the small plate with both hands. She needed to buy some time while she made a plan. "Excuse me?"

"I have a safe place prepared for you." John took a step toward her. "You must agree."

Determination and relief swept through her. John felt he'd succeeded in capturing her. She wouldn't submit to his act of coercion and violence. Nor allow him to harm anyone else.

"No!" She leapt to her feet, the cup and saucer clattering onto the low table, tea spilling across the silver tray. She summoned her magic as she surged in front of the table. "Ladies, stay behind me."

She lifted both hands, sparks at her fingertips. She crossed her arms and then waved them apart, pushing out a barrier around herself and the other women. The force of the expanding protective bubble knocked John backward with a cry of surprise, crashing backward and bumping his head against the wooden floor. Surprised but extremely glad to discover a new power, she augmented the force she applied until the barrier became impenetrable. The air around them pulsed with magic as she glared at the man intent on kidnapping her, all of them. She didn't mean him any lethal injury but she wouldn't stand by and let him hurt anyone else. After all, Haley and Tabitha were both witches as well. He'd want to remove them from the area just like her. She wouldn't allow it.

John shook his head, struggled to his feet. She glared at him all the harder. "Stay away. I won't let you harm any of us. I'll hurt you myself if it comes to that."

"Cassie, no!" Tabitha rose to her feet and held out a deterring hand. "Stop. He's trying to help."

The man had threatened them. She'd witnessed it for herself. Confusion and shock warred with the need to protect her friends from the hands of John Baker. She kept the barrier between them as she glanced at Tabitha. "Help? He's done nothing to stop the killings. We can't trust him." She turned back to John, fortifying the barrier with flames to keep him at bay.

"Cassie! This isn't the way." Tabitha eased toward her

within the protective bubble of the flaming barricade. "You must believe me. Hear him out."

Cassie focused on the woman. Tabitha meant what she said. She believed her husband wanted to help Cassie. "You're certain?"

Tabitha eased closer, one hand extended in a soothing gesture. "We've talked it out. It's all right."

Cassie met John's worried gaze, reaching out to find out his emotional state. The sense of success had vanished. He didn't look at her as if he'd bagged a trophy buck. Instead, his expression contained awe and respect with a smidge of fear for spice.

"Keep your distance." She relented, the flaming protective bubble vanishing into a shower of sparks. "What is this about?"

"I know who is behind the murders and he's targeting you." John held his hands out to either side of his body. "I'm glad you came to Riverwood. I hadn't anticipated your visit but it's perfect timing. Stay here where we can protect you."

"You know who it is? Who is it? We can put an end to all of this." Cassie gaped at him, trying to come to terms with the conflicting emotions roiling inside created from the deluge of information. The man they'd feared for so long now wanted to protect her? Mrs. Baker peered at her with a somber expression on her face. "If you truly know, then you should tell the sheriff so he can put an end to the killing."

"No, not yet. I intend to see an end to the man's actions but in my own way." He put up a hand to stop her from inquiring further. "You'll need to trust me on this, Miss Fairhope. I won't let him kill again, nor succeed in his aim of killing you. Your father will be here ere long and is fully capable of handling the issue. Without involving inept lawmen. I only ask that you remain here until your father returns to resolve the matter."

A spike of fear shot into her heart at his words. Surely her pa wouldn't take on a killer. Would he try to kill the killer? More bloodshed. She wanted an end to the violence, the fear, the threats. Perhaps her pa would use his magic to thwart all of it when he arrived. She held on to that hope as she swallowed the lump of fear in her throat.

"But why would I be safer here than in my own home with my brothers to protect me?" There she'd be surrounded by magical beings on guard and ready to defend her. But Riverwood? Tabitha and Haley hid their magic from John, kept it a secret out of fear of his reaction if he were to learn witches lived under his own roof. Haley had informed them months ago that he didn't cotton to witchcraft of any kind. "No offense, sir, but I do not understand."

"Nor do I, Father." Haley set the saucer she'd been clutching on the gleaming table, her eyes on her father. "What has changed?"

Mandy stood rigidly by the edge of the settee, her eyes alight with curiosity. "Pray tell us why we should believe any of this."

Tabitha made an elegant arc in the air with her fingers to gain Cassie's attention. "Let me explain. I've only recently learned that my dear husband has known about my magical proclivities, and of course of our daughter's as well. He's also aware of how special all of you Fairhopes are. I must confess to being surprised to learn that he'd known all along but chose to not make a fuss about it as long as I was circumspect in how and when I employed magic." She smiled up at her husband's loving expression as Haley gasped, covering her mouth with her fingers. "As a result of his confession and his concern for Cassandra's safety, I've placed wards around the house to keep out evil. We are all perfectly safe within these walls."

Cassie clapped a hand over her mouth. More secrets! Everywhere she looked she discovered somebody knew more about her own past than she did. Even their neighbor fathomed the truth clearer than she or her brothers. Their parents had done an excellent job of hiding the truth from them all of their lives. But to keep this from them, that John actually stood on their side not against them. That was too much. Wait until her pa got home. She had a few choice words for him.

"You knew, Father?" Haley rose from her seat to walk to her father's side and then wrapped her arms around him. "Why didn't you say anything earlier?"

"It didn't seem to matter." John smiled over his daughter's head as she hugged him. "I suppose it does after all. Now that it's all out in the open, there's no more need to act as if I don't like witches or witchcraft."

"But then where were you going at night?" Haley stepped away from her father to look up into his face. "I feared the worst."

"I did what I could to protect the women." He shook his head slowly, a flash of anger and regret in his eyes. "I didn't always succeed, of course, but I tried. He's been growing more angry and defensive and I do believe volatile. He's assigned several of his men to try to kill you, Cassie, which thankfully they've not succeeded in doing. I'm afraid he will. Thus my chat with Mrs. Baker about protecting you here until Reggie can do so."

Cassie reached out with her senses to determine his feelings, detecting his remorse and his anger and his concern about the killer.

"But Mrs. Baker, you created wards? All to protect me." Cassie sat back in her seat, as shock set her hands to trembling while she wrestled with the startling new information. "I hadn't considered invoking wards but that's a fine idea. Thank you."

"So now you understand." Tabitha folded her hands in her lap. "You must stay here for the few days until Reginald returns to use his immense powers to protect you and all the rest of us from this ever-growing group of men attempting to snuff us out like candles. Like you, Cassandra, we want to end the violence not perpetuate it."

"But I can't stay here. Nor can Mandy, she'll be missed at the inn." Cassie, too, had work to do: mending, preparing her garden for winter, entertaining the guests. And the preparations for the gathering in a matter of days as well. "Besides Giles will not permit it. He's probably on his way here now to check up on me."

"We'll let him know what's happening, naturally, but he can't let anyone know where you are." John strode over to the fireplace, holding his hands out to the snapping flames. "Mandy is free to leave as long as she keeps your secret. We don't want...the man responsible for all of this terror to sniff out your whereabouts and try again. Let him stew a bit before we put an end to his plans."

She stared at Tabitha for a long moment. "You believe I must stay here?"

"I do. We wouldn't have asked you to unless we felt it vital to your well-being." Tabitha reached out a hand toward Cassie. "I promise you'll be quite comfortable."

"Flint needs to know where I am and that I'm fine." She glanced at John. "He'll be frantic otherwise."

"I don't think it's a good idea." John turned his back to the fire to meet her gaze with dark eyes.

"I won't stay without letting him know where I am." Who knew what he'd do if she simply didn't come home for two days. The man would be beside himself and it would be all her fault. For keeping secrets of her own. No. "That's my condition for agreeing to this plan."

John studied her for what seemed a long time before nodding once. "As discreetly as possible, then."

"I know the perfect way to tell him." She only needed one thing. "Please open a window."

Chapter Sixteen

While Cassie was safely under Giles and Flint's protection in town, Silas stole a few minutes to go up to his mother's private attic to continue his research. The quiet space his mother created seemed like an ideal place to think through the information he'd unearthed so far. Tantalizing missing pieces to the puzzle of his family's past called to him. He'd read the published papers, the public acts reported for all to know, so next he'd focus on the private missives his ma had bundled and stored in the trunk. She must have saved them for a reason.

He lit the lamp and turned up the wick to increase the brightness in the room. Shining light on his mother's private lair, the place she came to work her magic. Her essence wafted from each artifact surrounding him. Had she imbued herself into the books, papers, lamp, furniture in general? Stamped her unique imprint on each of her possessions to lay claim on them forever? He cautiously picked up the casually draped blanket from the chair by the window and sniffed her special perfume. As before, echoes of her emotions filled him. His legs gave out and he sank onto the chair, the soft wool bundled on his lap.

Memories raced through his mind of running to throw his arms around her waist in a huge hug when she'd return from the market. He'd missed her sweet smile and the light floral scent she favored. Then, his little boy heart only knew her as a loving mother who took care of him when he was ill, soothed his misfortunes with a hug and a kiss on the head, encouraged his sense of adventure and creativity with a gentle nudge with her hand or her voice. The innocent love he'd put aside for years surged to the forefront of his memory. Tears smarted his eyes. He'd never hug her like that little boy again. He'd only ever see his mother as a ghost from now on.

Indeed, as he'd discovered the rest of his brothers also had experienced, she'd pushed him away, out of the nest as it were and into the big bad world to fend for himself as best he could. Bewildered, he'd struggled at first to find his feet but the road smoothed out once he linked up with a printer who needed someone to report on conditions in a neighboring town. He discovered he enjoyed being on the road to the next place and the next story. Without a home to turn back toward, he pushed forward to create a new path for his future. After all, there wasn't anything to look back on. Or so he thought until he'd answered Cassie's request to come to the inn. If it weren't for Cassie, he'd not have stayed in touch. He'd always had a special connection to her and made a point of sending her a note now and again. Deep inside, he'd needed to maintain a tie to his family however tenuous. Now he had a better understanding as to why.

Over the last several days he'd learned more and more about the kind of family he'd left behind. About his father's role in the rent in the family fabric. Giles had tried to help but as a boy he had to adhere to his father's rule. If anyone were to blame for George's death it seemed it was his pa. But somehow the pieces didn't make a complete picture. His father wouldn't harm anyone. Not the father he remembered as a youth. Reginald Fairhope was a man of honor and respect even if he could be rather selfish and self-serving at times. As in his insistence on supervising the furniture making. Silas had every intention of asking his pa one burning question: why did he stay away so long after Mercy's untimely death all because of furniture?

A family's safety and cohesion remained the father's highest duty. The patriarch ensured his wife and children had what they needed in terms of a safe place to sleep, food in their bellies, and protection against outside threats. At least, a decent father ensured those aspects of his charges' lives were met. His pa had left everything in the hands of a surrogate innkeeper. A young man who had no allegiance to the family and little if any experience in tending to a man's flock. Until he fell in love with his sister and then his interest escalated. Still, Flint's shoulders were not the ones destined to bear the burden of safeguarding the Fairhope legacy. Reginald's broader and more mature shoulders should carry the weight of that responsibility.

Heaving a frustrated sigh, Silas shifted to stare at the trunk and its cache of secrets hidden from view. For too long, the hopes and thoughts inside the trunks lay obscured. Time to bring them into the light. Without knowing what happened to cause the schism in the family tapestry they could never fully stitch it back together. Could never adhere to his mother's decree of stronger together if they remained divided and torn. He pushed to his feet, dropping the blanket over the chair, and strode to the trunk.

He raised the lid and lifted several beribboned bundles from the depths. Carrying them to the table, he stacked them beside the oil lamp. He smoothed out the blanket over the chair back, and then resumed his seat to begin sorting through the letters. Those written by anyone other than family he set aside, intending to go through them later. The first priority must be what the family had to say to each other.

Several letters came from his grandfather, Robert Covington, addressed in his flowing, looping script to Mercy Covington Fairhope. Including his surname—her maiden name—along with her married name indicated he wouldn't allow her to deny his parentage. Arranging the letters chronologically, he began reading. The import of each letter seared into his brain, the reiteration of Mercy's destiny and her role in the future of the family. Again and again, Robert insisted she do as he demanded: join with her sisters to create an all-powerful trinity of witches. Then they could serve to champion his desires in the region. To do his bidding. He insisted, cajoled, threatened her with every imaginable retribution if she didn't comply. If she allowed Hope's mediocre son to take her place, she'd never know a moment's peace. He declared he intended to assimilate her potentially powerful children into the family coven, how they'd become ever more powerful under his tutelage and guidance. The entire family would come together and be the most potent conclave of magical beings ever.

"Grandfather wouldn't take no for an answer." Silas stared at the handwriting on the page, absorbing the threat behind the words. His grandfather had a way with words, choosing them with a precision that lent power, weight, menace to each statement, each request, each demand. The old man did not appear dangerous in Silas' youth. Just another bearded relative who commanded attention and obedience.

"No, he wouldn't." Mercy shimmered into the room, hovering between the trunk and the table with its soft lamplight casting shadows across the floor. "Put those away, Silas. They're not something to share with anyone."

"Why didn't you say anything earlier about how Grandfather treated you?" His heart thudded in his ears, the risk his mother had faced down and pushed aside for years accelerating his pulse. "He seemed like just another overbearing father-figure to me when I was a boy. But this..." He flapped the pages of the last letter with a trembling hand. "He threatened severe punishment if you denied him."

Mercy shifted side to side for a moment and then calmed her agitation with a gentle smile. "He's no longer a threat to any of us, son. He died years ago."

"But his other daughters, your sisters, seem to want to carry on in his name." Silas folded the letter and shoved it back into its envelope. "What did he mean by not letting George take your place?"

"I'm not sure, actually. The boy didn't have the same proclivity toward magic as I do, even though I didn't want to use mine for dark magic. George couldn't have created the powerful trinity Father craved. But he could have with me, and ultimately the rest of you, under his command."

"So with George's death..." Silas tapped the corner of the envelope on the table as another piece fell into place. "They had leverage over you to live up to what he saw as your destiny, his demand for you to work with your sisters.

George died to force your hand? ”

She pressed her lips together for a long moment. “I suppose that's one way of looking at it. Or to make sure he didn't get in the way. Hope was understandably proud of her son. Hope wouldn't try to pull him into the trinity. Father wanted to make sure. Father believed it had to be three witches, no warlocks, to create the most powerful trinity. Hope didn't believe that, but she bent to our father's will after her son died.”

“Aunt Hope blames Pa for George's death, you know. She demands he apologize. But from what else I've learned, it seems that George died before his body surfaced so Pa couldn't have killed him.” Something clicked into place, but he withheld the suspicion from his mother. Would it make matters worse or better? Staring into his mother's wary expression, he decided to risk her ire. “Could someone have killed George as he dove into the water? Not merely allowed him to drown, as has been supposed, but actively worked to make sure he died and Pa blamed?”

Mercy frowned at him, shaking her head harshly. “Why?”

“Well...like you said, your father wanted George out of the running. Out of the way, as it were, and by blaming Pa, it might turn you back to your sisters' embrace.” Silas tapped the envelope three more times and then froze as he recalled the look in his aunt's eyes.

“What is it? Why do you look so horrified?”

Could she have done such a horrid thing to her sister, to her nephew? “Could Grandfather have asked Aunt Faith to ensure your role in the trinity?”

Mercy's frown deepened for a moment and then her eyes widened. “You think he had Faith kill George? Oh god."

A chill swept through Silas as horror spread across his mother's shocked features. "Well?"

"I think you're right. He'd use such machinations to achieve his desires." She slowly shook her head as her emotional reaction to such an atrocious act flitted across her face. "I can't believe I didn't see it sooner. Oh, Silas, you mustn't tell anyone. It will be bad all around."

His mother's sincere belief of the results of his grandfather's terrible manipulations rattled his certainty about telling the truth of the past. "I don't know, Ma, but I think it might help everyone if the real story of what happened were told instead of being kept secret."

"Sleep on it for now, please?" Mercy shimmered in agitation and upset. "I don't know how Hope would react to such news, or how Faith might retaliate for revealing her part."

"I suppose I can hold off for now..." Silas laid the letter on top of the stack as a wave of terror swept through him, coming from outside of himself. "I—"

"What now?"

He dropped the trunk lid closed with a bang. "It's Cassie. She's summoned Allegro. Giles isn't with her for some reason." He extinguished the lamp with a quick flick of his wrist. "I've got to go."

Allegro answered Cassie's silent call within a few minutes, swooping through the open parlor window. The other ladies pushed back in their chairs as he flapped around the room and then settled on her shoulder. John had left the room at the butler's summons. She stroked

Allegro's feathers, striving to stay calm. She was safe at Riverwood. Everyone said it was the right thing to do. She rolled a piece of note paper she'd dashed a few lines on into a scroll and tied a length of yarn around it.

"Take this to Flint." She held out the message and the falcon took it in his beak. "Thank you, Allegro."

With a tilt of his head and a flap of powerful wings the bird darted out the window and disappeared into the darkening sky.

If only she could fly home instead of hiding from the mysterious killer. It wasn't fair. She'd done nothing wrong. She'd done all she could to calm and encourage those around her. Yet she had to hide out like a criminal. It simply wasn't fair. She stared out the window as she blinked away tears.

"Everything will work out." Tabitha stopped beside her, a gentle hand on Cassie's shoulder. "Be patient."

She sniffled. "I'm trying."

"Your father will sort all this. Now, why don't we change for dinner. Haley can lend you something appropriate."

Footsteps in the passage announced John's return. "Look who I found at the door."

Cassie spun around to see Giles walk in behind her host. "I'm so glad to see you."

He'd only been behind her by minutes, and yet so much had changed.

"I see you made it here safely." Giles frowned as he approached her. "But why are you upset?

"Mr. Baker insists I stay here for my safety, under their protection until Pa comes home." Cassie searched her brother's eyes, looking for his reaction to her news. Not well.

"Here?" Giles peered at John, lifting his strong jaw as he regarded the older man. "She's under my protection."

"She'll be perfectly safe with me. As long as the killer doesn't learn of her whereabouts." John met Giles' antagonistic glare. "I promise."

"I've heard that before." He swung his head around to pin Haley with a scowl. "You promised me she'd be safe under your care. That you didn't plan anything unsavory. But it appears you're actually working with your father to entrap my sister, Miss Baker. I do not tolerate such deceit. Our engagement is off. I thought you were on our side."

"But, Giles..."

Haley stared at him, her heart in her eyes. Cassie dared not interfere when Giles' temper flared. Later she'd try to quell the misunderstanding. With luck, she'd help mend their relationship.

"I thought I had made it quite clear to you my feelings on this matter." Giles glared at John, while Haley was left to snap her mouth closed at the slight. "I'm taking my sister home. Do not try to stop me or you'll be on the receiving end of my fist." He took a step toward Cassie but John's words stopped him.

"It's for her own good, son. The men behind the murders are targeting witches and they've chosen Cassie to be next. They hope by killing her the rest will flee, the coven will disband."

Giles froze, staring at John. "You think she's a witch?"

"Come now, son, I know she is. Just like the rest of your family." John smiled, a friendly if wary lift of the corners of his mouth. "Your father told me everything before he left. How else would I know how best to watch over the family?"

"You know?" Giles studied him for several ticks of the

case clock. "You've known all along?"

"She must stay here for her safety. While she's under our protection she'll be fine." John swiveled to address Cassie. "You trust me, don't you?"

Cassie reached out to John, sensed sincerity and certainty. She glanced at Giles and nodded once. "I can tell he's being honest with us." Cassie crossed the room to stand beside Giles, comforted by both his presence and his bulk. "After being attacked in my own home, I'm inclined to believe Mr. Baker is right." Even if she wished he were not.

Giles angled to peer at her directly. "What are you suggesting?"

"I've agreed to stay." She held up a silencing finger as he made to continue. "Only for a day or two, though. Pa is due back and I must speak with him as soon as he arrives."

She'd pinned her hopes of a peaceable solution on his return. That he'd know how to confront her aunts, to deal with the dangerous men, and ultimately give his blessing for her and Flint to become united as man and wife. Her greatest wish remained to end the uncertainty, the threats, the fear, and the violence. She'd do whatever necessary to achieve that goal.

"I can't allow it." Giles crossed his arms over his chest, eyes dark and worried. "You should come back to the inn. You can't stay here by yourself."

Haley took a stride closer, dragging Mandy with her. "I'll be here for her, Giles. Along with my mother and father."

"That's not much reassurance after how you deceived me, Miss Baker."

She flinched at his words but stood her ground. "Nonetheless, she won't be alone."

John glanced between Giles and his daughter and then

back to Cassie. "A pair of days is all we need. Your father will arrive and then it will be safe for you to go home."

She detected no dissembling in his words or intentions. Cassie considered her brother. They all wanted the same thing. Her safety. The question of how to achieve it was the only sticking point. She had agreed to give John until her father came home. She snagged John's undivided attention with a lift of her chin. "You have two days and then I'm going home whether my father has arrived or not. Understood?"

"Yes, I understand." John bowed to her then straightened. "I appreciate your cooperation."

"Then I'm staying with you." Giles sidled closer to her. "Where you go, so do I."

Her brother, her Guardian. Pride and love mingled inside as she laid a hand on his tense arm in silent gratitude.

Cassie, are you safe? Where are you? Is Giles with you?

I'm at the Bakers' plantation with Giles. Do not worry. I'm fine.

That's a relief. I'm here if you need me.

Thanks. "Silas is aware of what's happening." She slid her gaze to meet Giles' tense glare. "Please, take Mandy back to the inn. Flint will know what's happening once Allegro delivers my note. I don't want him to worry."

"He has nothing to worry about since I'm sticking to you like tar." Giles wrapped a muscular arm around her shoulders. "Mr. Baker, you'll need to escort Mandy back to the inn. I'm not leaving my sister until she is safe."

"Thank you, Giles." Cassie peered up at her oldest brother, deeply grateful for his loyalty and strength.

"I'll take care of Miss Crawford, don't worry." John smiled gently at Mandy. "As soon as you're ready, I'll be delighted to take you home."

"Thank you for seeing to my safety as well." Mandy stood and dipped a curtsy.

"Now what?" Cassie glanced between John and Tabitha.

"Now we'll make you both comfortable for the next few days." John rubbed his hands together as he glanced around the group in the parlor, finally resting his gaze on Cassie. "Thank you for your trust, my dear."

Cassie had only agreed to stay because she sensed he spoke the truth and intended to help end the threat from the gang of men. He knew who the leader of the gang was but wasn't ready to point a finger at him. Yet. "Don't make me regret it, sir."

Chapter Seventeen

"That can't be." Flummoxed and angry, Flint glared at Daniel, Abram, and Mandy, all gathered around the bar. "Haley promised Cassie would be safe with her."

"Cassie sent you a note. Didn't you get it?" Mandy gripped the edge of the bar counter. "She is safe. That's why she's staying at Riverwood. Giles is staying with her, too. She's fine."

"How did she send me a note?" Flint stared at the girl as if she'd lost her mind. "Did you bring it with you?"

"Allegro left before Giles even arrived. I'd have thought he'd be here by now."

"I haven't seen him yet." Searing heat swept through his chest, leaving a trail of dismay and helplessness. At least Giles had elected to remain with her. That thought cooled the burning pain of her kidnapping, of essentially being held hostage. Even if she had agreed, she shouldn't have to avoid her own home, what should be her safe haven. The gang of men at the back of the dining room raised their voices as if excited and happy.

The only one missing was John. The man he'd once

thought responsible for the killings. Now to learn the opposite was true. He'd been doing what he could to protect witches, all of them. Including Cassie. Flint regarded the gathering of fifteen men, all with the appearance of upstanding citizens of the region. Counting among their number a couple of lawyers, several bankers, a handful of merchants, and a pair of clergymen. Yet they appeared to be the core of the threat to the region's witches.

"Klee! Klee!"

The falcon darted through the open window at the back of the dining room and flew straight to him. "Where have you been, Allegro?"

Allegro dropped a scroll of paper tied with yarn onto the counter. "Klee!"

Flint picked it up as the falcon hopped to one side, tilting its dark gray head with intelligent eyes. He pulled the yarn free, dropping it on the bar, and then unrolled the note.

My darling Flint,

I am writing to confirm for you that I am indeed safe here under Mr. Baker's protection. Mrs. Baker has protected the property with wards as a precaution. I love you and miss you. I promise to come home as soon as Pa is home. So be patient, my love. Please don't let anyone know where I am as Mr. Baker fears the killer may strike again if he knows.

All my love,

Cassie

"So you're correct, Mandy. She is safe." His stomach clenched against his need for action. Flint gestured to the hostess, flicking his hand toward the entrance to the dining room. "Since you're back, perhaps you can greet the new arrivals."

With a sigh and a quirk of her brows, Mandy stood. "Very well. Now you know she is fine, you needn't worry."

The girl's reassurance didn't lessen his anxiety over Cassie's situation. He fumed at the direction events had taken. He glared at her brothers, seated at the bar, eyeing him.

Anger burned his gut. Made him state his shock without thinking about consequences. "I can't believe John Baker would stoop so low as to kidnap my fiancé."

"Shh! Not so loud." Abram frowned at him.

Silence from the back of the room had Flint darting a glance to the gang of men. Their free-flowing banter and conversation had halted. They stared at him. Abram's warning came too late for his outburst. Damnation. He drew in a breath to calm the swirling anger making him reckless. He'd be more circumspect going forward, but what had he said that would cause the men such consternation? He replayed his statement in his mind.

"What is it?" Silas leaned on the counter, a slight frown dipping his brows.

The gang paid far too much attention to his business. A chill shivered down his spine. "The gang seems upset by the news of John's actions."

"Interesting." Silas swiveled to inspect the slowly sobering expressions of the large group of men, holding eye contact with them for several moments. Then he faced Flint again. "They are startled and worried. Why do you think?"

Flint lowered his voice to a whisper. "I wonder if they didn't know that John was working against them."

"That's very possible knowing what John has done." Daniel leaned back in his seat to study Flint. "John may have been staying involved in order to know what they planned so he could impede their misguided efforts."

Flint pressed his lips together to refrain from blurting out again what he thought he should do at that very moment. Mainly rush to Cassie and bring her home. Bring her back so he could guard her himself. His hand dropped from the counter to rest on the butt of the fancy flintlock pistol at his side. He'd vowed to protect her and he intended to keep his promise. Even as handicapped as he was without magic to ward off evil.

"No, don't." Silas shook his head at him, eyes knowing. "I know you want to. Pa will arrive shortly, if the sense of his happiness I'm feeling is right. Be patient."

"Patient? You realize the Allhallows gathering is in days, right? Cassie is in danger from those men. Her pa isn't here. The senator is coming in less than a week. There is much to be done, not least of which is bringing my girl home where I can protect her." Flint snatched the towel from its rail and scrubbed the bar surface. He needed action not patience. Visions of galloping to Riverwood flooded his brain, of carrying her home on his horse, one arm snugged around her as he brought her back to the inn and the rest of her family. "This is the time for doing."

"Not yet, but soon." Silas' gaze turned inward for a long moment and then his eyes trained on Flint. "Pa will be here and will have better options to share with us."

"I hope so." He flung the towel back over the rail and glanced at the gang again. They'd gone back to their conversation but more quietly than before. "*They* sure don't seem happy and willing to be patient."

Silas slid a glance at the men and then shook his head. "Maybe not, but there's nothing they can do right now. Not without drawing undue attention to their own activities."

"I should send for the sheriff." Flint bumped his fist on the bar. "If only they'd do something obviously incriminating so he'd have reason to arrest all of them."

"Well, we can't control what they do, but I have some things I need to take care of." Silas rose from his seat, pinning Daniel with his gaze. "I'm going to Ma's attic to work on the family history. I have a feeling we're going to need it. Once Pa arrives I won't have easy access to the attic and its papers like I do now."

"That's a good point. You go on and I'll see you later." Daniel lifted his ale and sipped. "Let me finish my drink and I'll come find you."

Mandy approached the bar, her expression guarded. "Flint, there's a man here says you ordered some things from town and he's brought them. He needs payment, though."

The supplies Cassie had ordered from town. She should be the one to receive them, to inspect them to ensure they were of the right quality and fashion. Instead, Flint would act as a poor substitute.

"All right." He met Silas' intense stare with a slight shake of his head. "Don't worry, I'm staying on the property even if I don't like the idea."

"It's what she wants." Silas laid his palms flat on the bar. "Only a couple of days and she'll be home. I'll go get her myself if necessary."

"I'll get her in two beats if you say the word." Daniel snapped his fingers. "Just give me a reason."

Flint held up a hand. "After what Mandy told us, I

suppose we need to trust that Cassie is reading John correctly and therefore knows what she's doing. Now, if you'll excuse me. After you, Mandy."

He turned and followed the hostess toward the entrance hall, and the man waiting there with his hat held between his hands. He spared a glance at Hope and Faith, seated at their usual table in the unusually quiet dining room since Cassie wasn't there to entertain the guests. The room seemed empty and sad without her energy and life. Rather the way he felt. They'd be sitting there waiting for her appearance for a long time but after his previous outburst he didn't dare relay the news to them in the public space. He nodded to them instead, tipping his fingers to his forehead before departing the room.

He approached the delivery man with hand extended. "I'm Flint Hamilton and I understand you have a delivery for me."

The man shook his hand and they discussed the payment and where Flint wanted the items deposited. The man set about bringing the barrels, crates, and burlap sacks onto the front porch while Flint strode to his office. Entering the small space, he was struck again by the realization that once Reggie returned it would no longer be his office. Reggie would take over the reins of running the inn and Flint would be relegated to...what? Manager? Or would he be let go entirely?

Stopping to survey the office, he drew in a long breath through his nostrils. He'd let Reggie down. Flint had failed in his aim of protecting the most precious possession of his boss: Cassandra. When Reggie returned and witnessed the mess of things Flint was about to hand over to him, he'd most likely fire him on the spot. Releasing the breath on a long sigh, Flint moved around the desk to write out a draft for the required amount. After he'd finished, he pulled out Cassie's note to read again. She asked the impossible.

"Patient? I am not patient!"

He flung the paper onto the desk and spun around as footsteps sounded from the family parlor. He wrestled his distress into a calm demeanor but it took all his emotional strength to do so. Keeping a brave and controlled attitude would instill more confidence in him, something necessary while running the busy and popular inn.

"I was just heading upstairs when I heard your declaration." Silas sauntered into the room with a grim smile on his lips. "You may be impatient, but you need to listen to my sister. Things will work out as they should."

"How can I be patient under these circumstances? Everything seems to be hanging in the balance, waiting for your father to arrive. He should have been here all along!"

"Calm down, Flint. He will be here soon. I can promise you that." Silas folded his arms. "Cassie says for herself she's fine, and I can sense that she is. I've reached out to her. Be patient and trust her. You must listen to her plea for patience."

"For her, I will try."

Flint suppressed a groan of remorse and frustration as he crossed to the office window to stare outside, across the carriageway and down the lane. Wishing with all his might he'd see Cassie riding home to him. He'd wait, perhaps not patiently but he'd do so. He could only hope he was doing the right thing by doing nothing as she'd requested.

I cannot believe I ever trusted the man. John Baker. He's

a snake in the grass. He will not succeed in his efforts to sabotage mine. I'll kill that young witch one way or another and then we'll take care of the rest of them one by one. But how? What would be the most effective and efficient way to remove the danger they represent? It should make a statement to all other witches. The inn is where they've been coming together, it should be where they die together. Ah. Yes. I know what I'll do. I'll trap them inside this very room, bring them all together, then burn it down.

The open house approached. They will be frolicking and having a merry time. They won't see their destruction coming. Rubbing my hands together, I only managed to keep from chuckling when I saw the inquisitive looks from the two crones at the front of the room. Let them look. Let them plan their festivities for Allhallows Eve. That will be the perfect night for their demise.

Writing down the legends of the wrath aimed at his ancestors placed a white-hot light on the animosity and fear others felt toward them. Silas hadn't anticipated the sense of dismay he'd experience with each stroke of his pencil. His grandfather had not been a nice man. He'd actively worked to broaden his territory of control and influence through any and all means necessary. Including to the ultimate detriment of his own family.

Silas held an affidavit of a man who claimed to the county judge that his grandfather had branded him as a coward after he refused to assassinate a rival. He stared at the damning words. How could his mother's father not only want a man to kill for him but then to apply a red-hot metal brand to the man's hand, a black "C" seared into his flesh?

Silas shuddered as the victim's experience flashed through him, the pain and humiliation and anger.

Laying the legal evidence aside, he scratched his pencil across the paper laying on the table by the open window in the attic. His mother's private space, where she kept all of her magical belongings and artifacts as well as the multitude of written evidence against the family. No wonder she hadn't wanted him to write down the truth of the family's history. But he must. The more he'd learned the more certain he became that his work would prove vital to the survival of the Fairhope family. Knowing where they came from would surely guide their future—both how they approached it, who they could trust, and what actions of the past they'd want to avoid repeating.

"What is that?" Mercy shimmered into sight by the Franklin stove, its gentle warmth pleasant on a cool late October evening. She glided over to peek over his shoulder at the words he'd written. "You wouldn't."

"I have and will continue to do so." He stared at the paper rather than up at his mother. He didn't need to see the dismay on her face having felt it flowing from her into his core. "It's imperative."

"No, it shouldn't be remembered but forgotten. Leave the past there." She sidled away, moving to peruse the books on the shelves on the wall. Then she spun around, her light blue dress swishing about her ankles. "Just ignore it. Burn it. We must move on if we're to find any means of coming together."

"We are coming together despite the family's history of violence and coercion." He looked up at her then, wishing he hadn't when he espied the worry and fear in her ghostly eyes. "Like you said, Ma, we're stronger together. But we must know our past in order to shape a future."

"What do you intend to do with those pages?" Mercy gestured to the stack of paper on the table. "You must know the truth doesn't always make things better."

He hesitated to answer her question as he sensed someone approaching, with both his inner senses and his hearing of footsteps on the stairs.

"Knock, knock." Daniel hesitated at the open door to the attic. "May I come in?"

Curiosity draped across Daniel's shoulders as Silas nodded at him. "I've been expecting you."

"Ma, you did a nice job of furnishing your little hideaway." Daniel strolled into the center of the attic to survey its contents. "Very cozy for such an intriguing spot."

"What do you mean by intriguing?" Silas sensed his surprise and delight overcoming any hesitation his brother had felt upon entering.

Daniel flung his hands out to either side as he pivoted in place. "It's not even visible from outside, this attic space. Ma, you did a fine job of creating your own enchanted haven."

"Thank you." She dipped a curtsy and then smiled at him. "I'm right proud of how it turned out."

Silas gawped at the pair grinning at him with a smug expression. He hadn't even processed the discrepancy. No one had mentioned the attic being an enchanted place to him and he just hadn't thought any more about the fact that the inn and residence were only two stories tall and yet...an attic was above his parents' bedchamber. Could the shimmering he saw and thought was a reaction to exhaustion have been magic? So much for being mindful and educated.

"Nonetheless, Ma, I intend to share what I've learned with the rest of the family." Silas lifted the papers and tapped them into an organized stack before placing them carefully on the table. "I may expand it into a book over time."

Daniel moved to the table and asked with an extended hand to read through the papers. Silas nodded and then addressed his mother while Daniel slowly flipped through the many carefully composed pages.

"You should want the rest of the family to know what your father had been doing. They will come together on your side of the issues once they fully understand just how dangerous a man, and powerful warlock, he was."

"But they may take everything out of context so that his actions seem even more vile than they really were." She drifted across the room, spinning about when she reached the open doorway. "He wasn't all bad. He was a loving father once..."

Silas angled his head briefly, peering at her. "Perhaps, but his actions in the years prior to his death speak volumes of how his intentions had become twisted and suspiciously aggressive. Like he wanted to control not only the territory in the county but the region."

Mercy shimmered and then calmed. "I think he did, honestly. I feared he did. He manipulated all of us to do his bidding, especially Faith apparently. I wasn't aware of that, but of his other desires and demands. That's when we made our decision to protect you all and remove you from within his grasp."

"Do your sisters understand that?" Silas stared at his mother's anguished expression. "I didn't think so. Perhaps they should be the first to read the family history I've compiled. Then they might give up their effort to recruit Cassie to their side and join us in fighting for our family."

Mercy shimmered with intense agitation again before sighing. "But you must share the story the right way, with respect and taking the proper precautions. Don't just spring the facts on them, you see?"

"I understand." Silas contemplated his mother for several beats of his heart. "I've decided that once Pa returns, and once Cassie is truly safe, it will be time for me to move on."

Mercy stilled, falling silent as she stared at him with sad eyes. "I'd hoped you stay like your brothers have chosen to do."

Silas firmed his lips as he gazed at his mother's ghost. He'd ventured to the inn at his sister's request in the vague hope of finding a way to reunite his family. By being willing to reunite with his sister, his father, and with any luck his brothers. Little had he realized he'd have the chance to rebuild his relationship with his mother...or her ghost at any rate. While he'd toyed with the idea of settling down like Giles had suggested, he couldn't. He simply wasn't ready to give up learning more about his country and the people in it. He needed to travel and see what was over the horizon.

"Pa is close. Once he's back and Cassie is safe and sound, then it will be time for me to go. Not before."

Daniel gazed at him over the handwritten pages. "I'm not surprised but I do hope you'll write to us, let us know where you are and how you fare."

"I will. I haven't found you all again to lose you." Silas tapped his pencil on the table for a moment and then laid it down. "Only after we've ended the threats will I pack my saddlebag and mount up. But there's work to be done before then.”

“Such as?” Mercy shifted, wrapping her arms around her waist.

“Completing what I started by coming here.” He’d finally figured out what his return meant for the family. Despite his mother’s reservations, he’d use his wordsmithing to repair his family. “To reunite us as one family, knowing our past, present, and hopes for the future. Only then can I move on.”

He’d craft a tale of dreams, desires, and dangerous demands. How they worked to force actions which forever changed the people involved. In order to make amends for past transgressions against the family, they’d all need to work to share openly and lovingly. They’d need to come together to be stronger.

“Oh, is that all?” Daniel tapped the stack of pages containing the details of the family’s past with his forefinger. “And you think your words can accomplish all that?”

“I do. But I guess we’ll have to wait and see, won’t we?” Silas let a sigh escape as he contemplated his ma and brother. “We’ll see what happens when Pa comes home.”

The End

Thanks so much for reading *Legends of Wrath*! The adventure continues, so stay tuned for more to come in this six-book series.

To find out about new releases and upcoming appearances, please sign up for my newsletter via my website at www.bettybolte.com. I send out a monthly newsletter with book news to share with my readers, upcoming events and signings, and even a few favorite recipes, puzzles, and other doings!

I'd love to hear from you! Feel free to send me an email at betty@bettybolte.com, find me on Facebook at AuthorBettyBolte, follow me on BookBub, or connect with me on Twitter @BettyBolte.

You can always find an updated list of the titles in this series, as well as all of my other books, at www.bettybolte.com.

Thanks again for reading!

Betty

About the Author

Award-winning author Betty Bolté is known for authentic and accurately researched historical fiction with heart and supernatural romance novels. A lifetime reader and writer, she's worked as a secretary, freelance word processor, technical writer/editor, and author. She's been published in essays, newspaper articles/columns, magazine articles, and nonfiction books but now enjoys crafting entertaining and informative fiction, especially stories that bring American history to life. She earned a Master's Degree in English in 2008, emphasizing the study of literature and storytelling, and has judged numerous writing contests for both fiction and nonfiction. She lives in northern Alabama with her loving husband of more than 30 years. Get to know her at www.bettybolte.com.

Be sure to check out materials for book club discussions at https://www.bettybolte.com/bookclub.

www.ingramcontent.com/pod-product-compliance
Lightning Source LLC
Chambersburg PA
CBHW021127190726
48288CB00008B/2534